111168

Published by LITTLE SIMON, a Simon & Schuster Division
of Gulf & Western Corporation,
Simon & Schuster Building, 1230 Avenue of the Americas,
New York, New York 10020

LITTLE SIMON and colophon are trademarks of Simon & Schuster
10 9 8 7 6 5 4 3
ISBN 0-671-45632-6

3/86 7.95 BT: City

Colour separations by
Newsele Litho Ltd., Milan, Italy.
Printed in Hong Kong by South China Printing Co.

Design by Dave Nash

For permission to include copyright material
acknowledgement and thanks for their help and courtesy
are due to the following authors and publishers:

Doubleday & Company, Inc. for *The Baker's Cat* from
''A Necklace of Raindrops'' by Joan Aiken. Copyright © 1968 by Joan Aiken;
Donald Bisset and Methuen Children's Books for *A Journey to the Sea*
from ''The Adventures of Yak'' by Donald Bisset;
Stephen Corrin and Faber & Faber Ltd for *The Ossopit Tree*
from ''Stories for Five Year Olds'' by Stephen Corrin;
The Bodley Head for *Lizard Comes Down from the North* from
''The Anita Hewett Animal Story Book'' by Anita Hewett;
Atheneum Publishers for *How the Whale Became* from
Ted Hughes, ''How the Whale Became and Other Stories''
Copyright © 1963 by Ted Hughes (New York: Atheneum 1963);
Franklin Watts, Inc. for *A Lion in the Meadow*
by Margaret Mahy. Copyright © 1969 by Franklin Watts, Inc.;
Faber & Faber Ltd for *Sam Pig and the Wind*
from ''The Adventures of Sam Pig'' by Alison Uttley.
All other stories in this book are retold from traditional sources
by Linda Yeatman and in this version are © Kingfisher Books Ltd.

A
Treasury of
ANIMAL
STORIES

Chosen and edited
by
Linda Yeatman

Illustrated
by
Hilda Offen

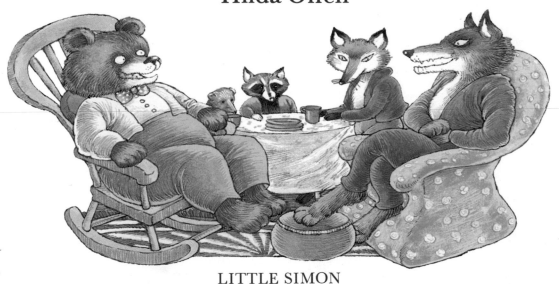

LITTLE SIMON

Published by Simon & Schuster, New York

Contents

The Old Woman and her Pig (6 minutes)   8
Traditional English

The Giraffe Who Saw to the End of the World (10 minutes)   14
Brian Patten

Lizard Comes Down from the North (12 minutes)   20
Anita Hewett

Anansi and Common Sense (4 minutes)   27
Traditional African and Carribean

Dick Whittington and his Cat (15 minutes)   30
Traditional English

The Little Red Hen and the Fox (5 minutes)   38
Traditional Irish and American

The Rats' Daughter (6 minutes)   42
Traditional Eastern

A Journey to the Sea (5 minutes)   46
Donald Bisset

Jerome, the Lion and the Donkey (10 minutes)   51
Early Christian Legend

The Tinder Box (15 minutes)   58
Hans Andersen

Country Mouse and Town Mouse (3 minutes)   67
Aesop

Elephant and Rabbit (5 minutes)   70
Traditional African

The Fox and the Crow (2 minutes)   74
Aesop

The Baker's Cat (15 minutes)   75
Joan Aiken

Henny Penny (3 minutes)   83
Traditional

The Fisherman's Son (10 minutes)   86
Traditional Caucasian

The Ossopit Tree (6 minutes)   92
Stephen Corrin

The Lion and the Mouse (2 minutes)   98
Aesop

The Dragon and the Monkey (5 minutes)   99
Traditional Chinese

Brer Rabbit Gets Himself a House (8 minutes)   102
Joel Chandler Harris

Puss-in-Boots (8 minutes)   107
Perrault

A Lion in the Meadow (4 minutes)   111
Margaret Mahy

The Black Bull of Norroway (10 minutes)   114
Traditional Scottish and Scandinavian

How the Whale Became (8 minutes)   120
Ted Hughes

The Traveling Musicians (6 minutes)   126
Grimm Brothers

The Little House (4 minutes)   131
Traditional Russian

Pegasus the Winged Horse (4 minutes)   134
Greek Legend

Sam Pig and the Wind (12 minutes)   139
Alison Uttley

The Little Jackal and the Crocodile (4 minutes)   148
Traditional African

The Great Flood (5 minutes)   153
Traditional – Bible and Fable

The Old Woman and her Pig

There was once an old woman who found some money under the floorboards of her house. "How lucky I am," she said. "I can go to the market and buy myself a pig."

So the old woman went to the market and bought herself a fine pig. Now it's easy to take a pig home from market if you have a truck, or even a cart, but the old woman had neither of these and so she had to walk home with the pig.

It was quite a long way and the road was busy, so she decided to take a short cut through the fields. But she had forgotten that there was a stile between two fields on her way and now, however hard she tried, the old woman could not make the pig climb over the stile.

The old woman saw a dog so she said,
"Dog! Dog! Bite the pig!
The pig won't climb over the stile,
and I shan't get home tonight!"

But the dog would not bite the pig.

Then the old woman saw a stick, and she said,
"Stick! Stick! Beat the dog!
The dog won't bite the pig,
The pig won't climb over the stile,
and I shan't get home tonight!"

But the stick would not beat the dog.

The old woman went a little further and she found a fire, and she said,
"Fire! Fire! Burn the stick!
The stick won't beat the dog,
The dog won't bite the pig,
The pig won't climb over the stile,
and I shan't get home tonight!"

But the fire would not burn the stick.

The old woman was getting very cross wondering how she was ever going to get the pig over the stile, when she saw a bucket of water. So she said,

"Water! Water! Put out the fire!
The fire won't burn the stick,
The stick won't beat the dog,
The dog won't bite the pig,
The pig won't climb over the stile,
and I shan't get home tonight!"

But the water would not put out the fire.

The old woman went a little further and she saw a bull standing in the field. So she said,
"Bull! Bull! Drink the water!
The water won't put out the fire,
The fire won't burn the stick,
The stick won't beat the dog,
The dog won't bite the pig,
The pig won't climb over the stile,
and I shan't get home tonight!"

But the bull would not drink the water.

The old woman went a little further and met a butcher. So she said,
"Butcher! Butcher! Kill the bull!
The bull won't drink the water,
The water won't put out the fire,
The fire won't burn the stick,
The stick won't beat the dog,
The dog won't bite the pig,
The pig won't climb over the stile,
and I shan't get home tonight!"

But the butcher would not kill the bull.

Then the old woman saw a rope, and she said,
"Rope! Rope! Hang the butcher!
The butcher won't kill the bull,
The bull won't drink the water,
The water won't put out the fire,
The fire won't burn the stick,
The stick won't beat the dog,
The dog won't bite the pig,
The pig won't climb over the stile,
and I shan't get home tonight!"

But the rope would not hang the butcher.

Then the old woman caught sight of a rat, and she called out,
"Rat! Rat! Gnaw the rope!
The rope won't hang the butcher,
The butcher won't kill the bull,
The bull won't drink the water,
The water won't put out the fire,
The fire won't burn the stick,
The stick won't beat the dog,
The dog won't bite the pig,
The pig won't climb over the stile,
and I shan't get home tonight!"

But the rat would not gnaw the rope.

The old woman wondered what on earth she was going to do when she saw a cat, and she said,

"Cat! Cat! Catch the rat!
The rat won't gnaw the rope,
The rope won't hang the butcher,
The butcher won't kill the bull,
The bull won't drink the water,
The water won't put out the fire,
The fire won't burn the stick,
The stick won't beat the dog,
The dog won't bite the pig,
The pig won't climb over the stile,
and I shan't get home tonight!"

The cat said, "If you bring me a saucer of milk I will catch the rat for you."

The old woman jumped for joy and ran over to a cow in the next field, crying, "Cow! Cow! Will you give me some milk for the cat?" and the cow said, "If you bring me some hay from that haystack over there I will give you some milk."

So the old woman fetched some hay for the cow and the cow let the old woman milk her. She took the milk to the cat and the cat lapped it all up.

Then the cat began to chase the rat,
The rat began to gnaw the rope,
The rope began to hang the butcher,
The butcher began to kill the bull,
The bull began to drink the water,
The water began to put out the fire,
The fire began to burn the stick,
The stick began to beat the dog,
The dog began to bite the pig,
The pig got a tremendous fright and leaped over the stile and the old lady got home that night.

The Giraffe Who Saw to the End of the World

Brian Patten

In a jungle that was almost a forest, and in a forest that was almost a wood, and in a wood that was almost a garden, there once lived an elephant and a flower and a pig and a giraffe and a kuputte-bird. There was also a hyena there and a plinkinplonk and monkeys as well; and of course there was a forest of moonbeams, and a silver ant that dreamed of silence, and a river that told the strangest stories.

Sometimes the giraffe came to the hill where the elephant and the flower lived. The giraffe had a very long neck, and when it stood on top of the hill and stretched its neck it could see over the trees and mountains to the end of the world.

One day the flower asked, "What is the end of the world like?"

"Beautiful," said the giraffe.

"What lives there?" asked the elephant.

"Giraffes, of course," answered the giraffe.

The elephant had always thought elephants lived at the end of the world. And the flower had always thought only flowers could live in such a faraway place.

"Isn't there even one elephant there?" asked the elephant.

The giraffe stretched its neck as hard as it could. It looked across the trees and the mountains for a long time, and then said, "No, only giraffes."

"Maybe the giraffes are hiding a few flowers," suggested the flower.

"Most certainly not," said the giraffe.

"He's not telling the truth," said a voice above them. It was the sparrow, who had been sitting all the time on the giraffe's head. "I can see the end of the world a little better than he can, and it's full of sparrows. Very large sparrows, even larger than eagles."

The giraffe said it had forgotten to mention sparrows, as they were smaller than giraffes.

"But there are definitely no elephants or flowers there," it insisted.

"You're quite right," agreed the sparrow.

The elephant and the flower decided to go for a walk instead of listening to the other two creatures, who were now boasting loudly. On their walk they asked all the creatures they met, "What do you think lives at the end of the world?" And the ant-eater said ant-eaters, and the snake said snakes, and the pig said pigs and the lizard said lizards. And every single creature thought the only things that lived at the end of the world were just like themselves, only a little larger.

Later in the afternoon when the elephant and the flower returned to the hill, they found all the creatures they had met on their walk gathered around the giraffe. The giraffe and the sparrow had agreed that only giraffes and sparrows lived at the end of the world. They were telling the other creatures that there were lakes and forests and rivers and trees and even weeds there. But no other animals.

The animals were very indignant. "We want to see for ourselves," they shouted.

"You can't," said the giraffe. "You're not tall enough."

"You can't," said the sparrow. "You've got no wings."

Then the pig had one of its rare ideas. "We'll all climb up the giraffe's neck and see for ourselves," it said.

The giraffe didn't like the idea, especially as it was the pig's.

"It's a stupid idea," it said. "Fancy a pig trying to make a suggestion of any kind. It's bound to fail."

But the other animals did not agree. They wanted to see the end of the world for themselves and they shouted and grunted so much that the giraffe had to agree to the pig's idea.

So first the snake climbed up. "Just as I thought," it said. "The end of the world is full of snakes."

"Nonsense," squeaked the pig, and he began to climb up the giraffe, slipping every now and then. He clung to the giraffe's ears and shouted down: "The snake's lying as usual. The end of the world's full of pigs. Very beautiful pigs. I can even see a King Pig sitting on a throne."

"Rubbish," shouted the ant-eater. "Let's have a look."

And when the ant-eater had reached the top it said, "Why what glorious ant-eaters there are! And so many ants to eat as well."

"I still think that they're all wrong," said the sparrow who was fluttering above the ant-eater. "I'm the furthest up, and so have the clearest view. It's definitely sparrows."

And so the creatures began to argue.

"High up is far enough up to see the end of the world," they shouted at the sparrow. And the pig was so angry it nearly fell down.

"Take your feet out of my ears," it squeaked at the ant-eater, who was sitting unsteadily on top of it. "And take your hoof off my head," shouted the snake.

As they argued, other creatures began to climb up the giraffe's neck. For miles and miles around, the jungle was full of talk and speculation about what lived at the end of the world.

Soon there was a gigantic pile of creatures on top of the giraffe's head. There were snakes and ant-eaters and pigs and frogs and monkeys and the white rabbit as well. Only the larger jungle creatures stayed on the ground with the elephant and the flower. They thought it a rather undignified heap, and knew quite well what lived at the end of the world.

The giraffe's neck was beginning to ache and strain.

All the time the creatures had been clambering over each other, a caterpillar had been slowly working its way up the giraffe's neck. It climbed on to the pig's head and stood upright. It was a very timid caterpillar and was a bit afraid of saying that the world was full of caterpillars. But it didn't have to anyway. The weight of all the creatures had become too much for the giraffe. It staggered on its feet, then tumbled down the hill. The creatures fell down on top of it in a huge heap. They all wriggled and groaned. And when they had untangled themselves they surrounded the caterpillar.

"It's your fault," said the pig. "It was your weight that made us fall. Now you'll have to settle the argument."

The caterpillar was very afraid of the animals, and it didn't want to make them any angrier by saying the end of the world was full of caterpillars.

So it said: "The end of the world's full of everything."

Though the other creatures did not believe it, they were so relieved that it wasn't full of caterpillars they agreed that maybe the caterpillar could see best after all. And so they went home happy, leaving the flower and the elephant alone on the hill. It was getting dark anyway.

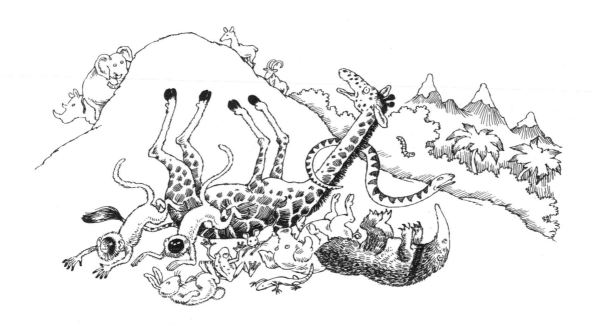

Lizard Comes Down from the North

Anita Hewett

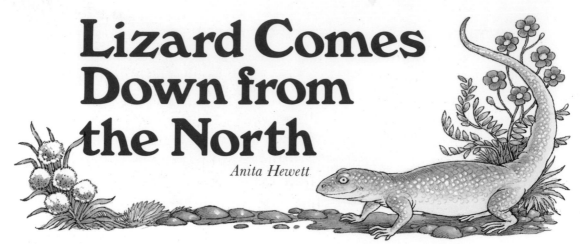

"Happy days!" said the little green Lizard, flicking his tiny tail in the air. "I'm going to the forest. Oh, happy days!"

And he pattered along on his stumpy legs.

"It's a long, long journey I'm making," he said. "Over bushland and sand and grassland and scrub."

And he hopped in the air with a squeak of delight, because he felt gay and brave and adventurous.

Then Lizard looked up against the sun, and far above him the black-feathered swan beat his wings in the air, and called: "Why are you coming down from the north, you strange little thing with a scaly back?"

But Lizard heard only the beat of strong wings as Swan flew away. So on he pattered.

Black Swan came to the sandy desert.

"I mustn't fly over the sand," he said and he called to Kangaroo Mouse below, "Mouse-with-a-pocket, take my message. Go to the forest and tell them there that a creature is coming down from the north. He has scales on his back, and a flicking tail and he's walking along on his sturdy legs."

Mouse jumped away towards the forest. Faster and faster and faster she raced, until at last her spindle-thin legs were springing so fast that they could not be seen, and she seemed to be a ball of fur, twirling and whirling and blown by the wind.

Then Kangaroo Mouse reached tussocky grassland and stopped. She sat by a tuft of grass and said:

"It's twice as tall as myself *and* my tail, and it's thick and prickly. I can't go on. These kind of jumps are for *real* kangaroos."

"Did you call me?" asked Kangaroo.

"No," said Mouse. "But I'm glad you're here. Go to the forest and take my message. A creature is coming down from the north. He has big shining scales and a beating tail, and he's walking along on his big strong legs!"

Kangaroo leaped towards the forest, crushing the grass beneath his feet. He came to the scrubland, and there he stopped. He saw spiky thickets, and thorny stems.

"Cassowary!" Kangaroo called. And out of the scrub came the great black bird. "Cassowary, take my message. A creature is coming down from the north. He has great shining scales, and a huge beating tail, and he's marching along on his mighty legs."

Cassowary turned to the scrub. He was not afraid of its spikes and thorns.

"I'm a fighting, biting, battling bird. I can push through worse than this," he said.

He pushed and kicked through the spiky scrub, until he saw the forest ahead. He ran through the trees, and before very long he saw Bower Bird, Possum, Platypus, Turkey, and Wombat.

"Listen," he said. "Here is my message. A creature is coming down from the north. He has huge shining scales, and a great lashing tail, and he's crashing along on enormous legs."

The creatures stared at each other, and trembled.

"It's a dragon," said Bower Bird.

"He'll eat us," said Possum.

"Help!" said Platypus.

"Save us," said Turkey.

"What a hullaballoo," said Wombat.

Cassowary stamped his foot.

"You make me angry, you foolish creatures. Talking will do no good," he said. "Why don't you stir yourselves up, and *do* something?"

And he stamped away angrily back to the scrub.

"We must frighten the dragon away," said Bower Bird.

"We must make a scarecrow to scare him," said Possum.

"We don't want to scare a *crow*," said Platypus.

"Then we'll make a scaredragon," Turkey said.

"What a to-do and a fuss," said Wombat.

They stuck the branch of a tree in the ground, for the scaredragon's body. Then they stuck a pineapple on to the branch, for the scaredragon's head.

But still they felt frightened.

"We must hide behind a wall," said Bower Bird.

"And look out over the top," said Possum.

"And when we hear the dragon coming, we'll shout, and wave our paws," said Platypus.

"And make our faces look fierce," said Turkey.

"What a hurry and a scurry," said Wombat.

The creatures began to make a wall.

They stuck a row of sticks in the ground, and Bower Bird, who knew about such things, fixed creepers and stems and twigs between them.

Possum banged the wall with his paw, to see if it was strong and safe.

Platypus filled the cracks with mud.

Turkey scraped up a pile of leaves, building them up behind the wall.

Wombat ran around in circles.

"Now we *ought* to be safe," they said.

They stood in a row on the pile of leaves, looking out over the top of the wall.

And they waited, and waited, and waited.

Into the forest came little green Lizard, flicking his tiny tail in the air.

"Happy days!" he smiled to himself. "I've come to the forest. Oh, happy days!" And he pattered along on his stumpy legs.

"It's a long, long journey I've made," he said. "Over bushland and sand and grassland and scrub."

He hopped in the air with a squeak of delight, because he felt happy and safe and friendly.

Then Lizard looked up.

He saw the scaredragon.

"What is that pineapple doing?" he said. "Just sitting quite still, all alone, on a stick?"

He saw the wall, and over the top of it, the faces of Bower Bird, Possum, Platypus, Turkey, and Wombat.

"And what are *you* doing, up there?" he asked.

The five faces stared back at little green Lizard.

"We're hiding away from the dragon," said Bower Bird.

"He's coming down from the north," said Possum.

"He'll eat us all up if he can," said Platypus.

"He has huge shining scales and a great lashing tail, and he's crashing along to the forest," said Turkey.

"*What* a time we've had!" said Wombat.

Lizard's small scales shone green in the sun as he flicked his tiny tail in the air. Then he pattered behind the wall, and said:

"Please may I hide behind your wall? I'm not very fond of dragons myself."

So Bower Bird, Possum, Platypus, Turkey, Wombat and Lizard looked out over the top of the wall, waiting for the dragon to come.

And they waited, and waited, and waited.

Far away, a dead branch fell, crashing down to the forest floor.

"The dragon! It's coming," the creatures cried.

They shouted, and flapped their paws about, and made fierce faces, until they were tired.

Then they all said: "Sh!" and "Listen!" and "Hush!"

They kept very still behind the wall, and the only sound they heard was a plop! as a ripe red berry fell to the ground.

"Hurrah!" cried Bower Bird. "We've done it! We've done it! We've scared the dreadful dragon away."

"He's crashing back to the north," said Possum.

"He'll never come *here* again," said Platypus.

"We're really rather clever," said Turkey.

"Clever and brave and fierce!" said Wombat.

Lizard did not say a word. He had disappeared behind a tree.

He looked at his little shining scales, and his flicking tail, and his stumpy legs.

He looked and he thought very hard.

And he guessed.

"Oh my, I'm a dragon, I am!" he said. "Oh ho! I'm a dragon. A great fierce dragon!"

Then Lizard flicked his tiny tail, and he rolled on the ground with his legs in the air, laughing and laughing and laughing.

Anansi and Common Sense

Y ou may already know that Anansi is a spider, an impudent spider, full of tricks and surprises, but did you know that Anansi is responsible for the fact that everyone – or almost everyone – has a little bit of common sense? This is how it happened.

Anansi was feeling full of importance one day, and thought the cleverest thing he could do was to collect up all the common sense in the world and keep it safe in one place. So he scuttled here and scuttled there, gathering it up in a great calabash. He then plugged the calabash with a roll of dried leaves.

"There," he said to himself; "is all the common sense in the world. Whenever I need it I shall be able to help myself, and my enemies will have none. I *shall* have fun for I shall always get the better of them." He really was pleased with himself.

"Hey, wait a minute though," he thought, "where can I keep it safe? Everyone will want to steal it from me. I know, I'll put the calabash at the top of that great coconut tree. None of the other animals will ever find it."

So Anansi got a long rope and tied it around the calabash, and then he looped the other end of the rope around his head. The calabash hung down in front of him, leaving all his legs free to climb the tree.

Well, Anansi started to climb the tree, but it was not easy as the calabash kept bumping around between him and the trunk of the tree. Slowly he inched up on his eight legs until, suddenly, when he was about half way up, he heard laughter below on the ground.

Now there is nothing Anansi hates more than being laughed at. Looking down he saw a small boy and the small boy was laughing his head off.

"Fancy climbing a tree with the calabash in front of you, Anansi!" he called out. "Surely you know that if you want to climb a tree with a calabash, it is more sensible to put the calabash on your back."

Anansi quivered with annoyance, in fact he was furious, for what the small boy said was common sense, yet hadn't he, Anansi, collected all the common sense in the world and stuffed it into the calabash?

In a rage he flung the calabash to the foot of the tree, where it shattered. The common sense inside was scattered into little pieces and blown all over the world, and everyone, or nearly everyone, got a little bit. So when you show you have some common sense, remember you have Anansi the Spider to thank for it.

Dick Whittington and his Cat

There was once a poor boy called Dick Whittington who lived in a small village in the south of England. He had no proper home for both his parents had died, and he was unkindly treated by many of the villagers. One day, Dick overheard someone say that the streets of London were paved with gold, and he decided that he would go there at once and pick his fortune up in gold pieces from the streets, for he thought people might treat him more kindly if he were rich.

So young Dick set out to walk to London. He had not gone far when a man in a cart stopped and asked him if he was running away from home. "I have no home," Dick answered. "I am on my way to London to find my fortune."

"I'm going to London myself," said the carter. "Jump up here beside me and we will journey together."

They arrived in London just before nightfall, and the carter left Dick and made his way to an inn. Poor Dick stood alone and looked around him in dismay. Where was all that fine gold? All he could see were dirty streets and lots of unfriendly people. He had nowhere to sleep and in the end he spent the night in the corner of an alley where he hoped he would come to no harm.

The next morning Dick woke up cold, miserable and very hungry. He wandered around begging for food, but again and again people shouted at him, "Go away you lazy rascal! Be off with you," and aimed angry blows at his head. At last he collapsed in the street, and lay there, too weak to look further for food.

By chance, Dick had fallen in front of a house belonging to a rich merchant called Mr Fitzwarren. The cook was trying to drive Dick away, when Mr Fitzwarren returned home from inspecting his ships. He stopped and said to Dick, "Why don't you work if you need food?"

"I would work," said Dick, "but I know nobody who will give me anything to do."

"Take him into the kitchen," Mr Fitzwarren ordered the cook. "Feed him first and then find some work for him."

So Dick was given a home and a living. He had a small corner of the attic to sleep in and his job was to help the cook with all the pots and pans in the kitchen. Dick's life should have been much better than before, but he still had two difficulties to face.

The first was that the attic he slept in was overrun by rats and mice. At night they scampered all over him and kept him awake. After a time he solved this problem by saving the few pennies he was paid, and buying himself a cat. In no time at all, the cat chased away all the rats and mice and Dick was able to sleep peacefully.

The other difficulty, which was not so easy to overcome, was the cook's bad temper. She shouted and screamed all day, and would scold Dick and hit him with a wooden spoon, even when he was working as hard as he could.

One night Dick decided he could stand it no more. Early the next morning before the cook was up, he set out with his cat to seek his fortune elsewhere. The two of them walked as far as Holloway, on their way out of London, then Dick sat down on a stone to rest. It was the first of November, All Saints' Day, and the church bells were ringing. As Dick sat and listened it seemed they were ringing out a message for him:

Turn again Whittington,
Thou worthy citizen,
Lord Mayor of London.

"Lord Mayor of London?" said Dick. "I should like to be Lord Mayor and ride in a fine coach. I can put up with a few scoldings from the cook if that is what is in store for me." So Dick and his cat retraced their steps to Mr Fitzwarren's house. Luckily they were able to slip back before they had been missed.

Now Mr Fitzwarren used to send ships far across the sea to trade with other countries. He would load a ship with goods for the captain and ship's crew to sell in faraway places and then they would bring back goods that could be sold at home.

One day he called his household together. "I am sending a ship to the African coast to trade," he said. "Would any of you like to send something of yours on it? You can then share in the profits if the voyage is successful." Everyone produced something except for Dick, who had nothing to offer. "Have you nothing of your own, Dick?" asked Mr Fitzwarren kindly, and Dick replied, "Only my cat."

"Then let your cat go on the ship," said Mr Fitzwarren. His daughter, Alice, said, "Dick loves his cat. Let me put something in for him." But her father said, "No, it must be his, not something belonging to someone else."

So Dick fetched his cat and said goodbye to it sadly. The captain of the ship was delighted, for the cat was an excellent mouser, and so he had no trouble with rats and mice on his voyage.

After some months the ship arrived at a place on the African coast called Barbary, where people called the Moors lived. The captain sent a message to the king to say he had fine goods for sale, and he was invited to the palace to show them. While he was talking to the king and queen some dishes of food were brought in, but almost immediately rats and mice ran up and, before the captain's eyes, ate all the food. The captain was astonished, and asked if this was what normally happened.

"Alas, yes!" came the reply. "The country is suffering from a plague of rats and mice, and we cannot get rid of them."

"I think I may have the answer on my ship," said the captain, and he sent a message asking for Dick's cat to be brought to the palace. More food was laid out, and the rats and mice appeared as before. The cat immediately pounced, killing at least a dozen before they scattered. Everyone was delighted, and the queen asked, "What do you call this animal?"

"Puss is the name she answers to," said the captain, and when the queen called, "Puss, puss," the cat went over to her and purred. The queen was a little alarmed at first, as she had seen how fiercely the cat had attacked the rats and mice, but the captain told her not to be anxious. "Puss is very friendly with people," he said, "and would soon rid your kingdom of rats and mice."

"I would give great wealth to own this animal," said the queen.

So the captain began bargaining, and it was agreed that the
king would buy the whole cargo from Mr Fitzwarren's ship and
pay a fine price for it, and for the cat alone the king paid ten times
the sum again.

When the ship came back to the Port of London, the captain
showed Mr Fitzwarren the gold and jewels he had brought from
Barbary and told him the story of the cat. The merchant sent for
Dick. "From now on, Dick," he said, "we should all call you Mr
Whittington, for you are a rich man." Mr Fitzwarren then paid
him all the money the captain had received for the cat.

From this time on Dick worked with Mr Fitzwarren, and became a successful merchant himself. He married Mr Fitzwarren's daughter Alice, and three times he was elected Lord Mayor of London. He was also in time knighted by the king and became Sir Richard Whittington. He was not only famous, but he was popular too for he always helped the poor with his money. Sometimes when he was old he would tell his grandchildren the story of his cat, and how the bells of London had called him back when he was only a poor boy:

Turn again Whittington,
Thou worthy citizen,
Lord Mayor of London.

The Little Red Hen and the Fox

Alittle red hen lived all alone in a house in the forest. She was a houseproud little hen who always kept her house neat and tidy. She always wore an apron and in the pocket she kept scissors and a needle and thread, for she always said, "You never know when they will come in handy."

Now the little red hen had one enemy – a rascally fox who lived over the hill. The fox used to lie awake at night thinking how much he would enjoy eating the little red hen. She took great care not to fall into any of the fox's traps when she was out in the forest during the day, and in the evening she always stayed at home. What is more, she always locked her door when she went out and slipped the key into her pocket with the scissors and needle and thread, so that the greedy fox could not creep into her house. She locked the door behind her too, whenever she was inside the house.

The fox used to watch her from behind a tree, and one day he said to his old mother who lived with him, "Mother! Stoke up the fire, and keep a big pot boiling, for tonight I am going to catch the little red hen. I have worked out a plan which will not fail." He took a sack, slung it over his shoulder, and set out over the hill to catch the little red hen.

He crept as close as he could to the little red hen's house, and there he lay in wait. Sure enough, before he had been there an hour, the little red hen came out.

She was just going to the wood pile to bring in some wood, so she did not bother to lock the door behind her. Quick as a flash that old rascal the fox was inside her house with his sack, and was waiting for her as she returned with some sticks. "Hello there, little red hen," he called out as she shut the door. "I have caught you now, and you are coming home with me for my supper!"

With a flurry of feathers and a great deal of squawking, the little red hen flew out of the fox's reach, and settled on some rafters above his head.

"Don't you be so sure of yourself you old rascal," said the little red hen. "You can't reach me up here."

That was true. The fox sat down wondering what to do next, and all the while the little red hen sat up in the rafters hoping the fox would get bored or hungry and go and look for his supper elsewhere. But foxes are not called cunning for nothing, and the old rascal now thought of a way to bring the hen down from the rafters.

He started to twirl and turn, round and round, chasing his own tail. Faster and faster he went until the whole house seemed to be full of twirling red fox.

The little red hen grew so dizzy watching him spin that she lost her balance and fell off her rafter with a great thud. In a trice the fox bundled her into his sack, flung it over his shoulder and set out over the hill to his home.

At first, the little red hen was confused by her dizziness and the fall, and by the darkness in the sack, but her mind soon cleared, and she lay quietly waiting for a chance to escape.

The fox, even though he had succeeded in bringing the little red hen down off the rafters, was still feeling quite dizzy and breathless from all that spinning around. So on the way home he sat down for a rest and put the sack on the ground beside him. In no time at all, the little red hen had taken her scissors from her pocket and snip, snip, snip, she cut her way out of the sack. She saw a stone nearby and rolled it into the sack and, while the fox was lying back chuckling to himself, the little red hen stitched up the hole. She finished sewing and just had time to hide behind a tree before the fox took up the sack once more and hurried on over the hill to his own house.

"Here I am, mother," he called, as he came into his house. "Is the pot boiling? The little red hen is in the sack."

"Everything is ready," replied his mother. "Put the hen straight into the boiling water."

"Here she comes," said the fox, as he opened the sack and emptied it into the cooking pot.

Splash! The stone fell into the water.

"That's a very odd hen," shrieked the fox's mother. "How dare you fool me like that!" But the fox knew that it was he who had been fooled by the little red hen.

He and his mother went to bed hungry that night, and the next day the fox went hunting for his supper in a different direction. As for the little red hen, she went home and, for the rest of her days, she always carried a pair of scissors and a needle and thread in her pocket, and she would always say with a smile, "You never know when they will come in handy."

The Rats' Daughter

Mr and Mrs Rat had the most beautiful daughter. She had the longest slinkiest tail you could imagine, and the most remarkable long, elegant whiskers. Her silky coat was a lovely glowing pinkish brown color, and her teeth were gleaming white with sharp points. She was in every way a very lovely young rat.

Mr Rat was hoping to find a handsome young rat as a husband for his daughter. Mrs Rat, however, was more ambitious and hoped to marry her daughter to the most powerful creature in the world.

"I have been thinking, my dear," she said to Mr Rat one day, "that there is nothing more powerful in the world than the Sun. I feel sure the Sun would like to marry our lovely daughter."

Mr Rat was rather taken aback by this idea, but seeing that his wife's mind was made up, he agreed. So they all set off to call on the Sun.

Now the Sun was not at all interested in the idea of marrying a rat – even a very beautiful rat, but he listened politely to what the parents had to say, and thought for a few moments before replying.

"You flatter me when you say I am the most powerful thing in the world, for I am not as powerful as that Cloud over there. He can stand in front of me, and shut off my light and heat whenever he wants. I think your daughter would do better to marry the Cloud."

Mr and Mrs Rat were delighted with his suggestion, for they could see at once that what the Sun had said was true. Certainly the Cloud was more powerful than the Sun, for at any time he could cover the Sun whether the Sun wanted it or not. "We should go to the Cloud with our daughter," they agreed, "and offer him the chance to marry a bride of the greatest beauty."

The Cloud was rather surprised when Mr and Mrs Rat called on him to offer him their daughter's hand in marriage. He agreed with them that she was indeed a most beautiful rat, but he did not like the idea of marrying her at all. He considered carefully before replying.

"My friend the Sun is kind to describe me as the most powerful thing in the world but I'm afraid he's mistaken. The Wind is far more powerful than I am. The Wind can blow me across the sky at a moment's notice. I think you should call on the Wind and suggest he marries your daughter."

Mr and Mrs Rat saw at once that what the Cloud said was true so they took their daughter to visit the Wind.

The Wind stopped blowing for a few minutes to talk to the Rat family, but he did not like the idea of marrying at all. He was far too busy to stay still in one place for long.

So the Wind said to Mr and Mrs Rat:

"The Cloud was right to say I am more powerful than he, but have you considered that the Wall over there is more powerful than me? However hard I blow, I can never blow him down. I think you should take that beautiful little daughter of yours to him. He is the most powerful of all."

The Wind, who was unused to staying still even for a few minutes, rushed off, leaving Mr and Mrs Rat nodding at his wisdom. "Come along child," they said to their daughter, "We will go and see the Wall. He will surely be glad to have such a beautiful bride."

When they arrived at the Wall, Mr and Mrs Rat bowed low before him, for they could see he was extremely strong and powerful. They explained that they had come to offer him their beautiful daughter as a wife and the Wall replied that he would think over the idea very carefully. But while he was thinking, there was a sudden and unexpected interruption.

"I don't want to marry a Wall," shouted Miss Rat, twitching her whiskers and stamping her foot. "I would have married the Sun, or the Cloud, or the Wind, but I don't want to have a Wall for my husband," and she burst into tears.

Mr and Mrs Rat were horrified at their daughter's rudeness, but the Wall said with great tact, "Your daughter is right. She should not marry me. I am certainly more powerful than the Wind who cannot blow me down, but there is something even more powerful than me. There is only one animal who can turn my strength into nothing, who can reduce me, a Wall, into dust. That animal is the Rat, who can gnaw through me with his sharp teeth. I would advise you to marry your daughter to the finest rat you can find. She will never have a more powerful husband."

And so it ended happily. Mr Rat was glad because he had always thought there was no finer creature on earth than the Rat. Mrs Rat was pleased now that she knew how powerful a rat husband would be. As for the Rats' Daughter, she was delighted. She did not want to marry the Sun or the Cloud or the Wind or the Wall, but she thought she would be very happy indeed married to a handsome young rat.

A Journey to the Sea

Donald Bisset

Yak was waiting for the morning. He heard the tinkling of a bell in the monastery, nearby.

Every morning, while it was still dark, he could hear it. Small white snowflakes fell out of the dark on to his long warm hair. Gradually the sun rose. For a moment all was still. Then, out of the grayness floated a seagull.

"Yark!" it cried.

"Mrmph!" replied Yak.

Which is a sound very like cows make while they are waiting in the meadows to be taken home at milking time.

Mocka, the seagull, landed on a rock close by.

Now it was morning.

Mocka was Yak's friend, who lived by the sea.

How Yak longed to go to the seaside. Mocka had told him about the children with buckets and spades on the beach. About the waves that rolled ashore every moment, hour after hour, day after day, year after year for a thousand million years, way beyond the edge of time.

Mocka hopped from the rock and laid something among the stones by Yak's hooves.

It was a seashell. A lovely spiral seashell.

"For me?" Yak looked at him. He put his ear by the shell and heard, as from far away, the hiss and murmur of the sea.

"Yark!" went Mocka – and flew away.

Yak tilted his head and hooked the shell on to one of his horns. Then pressed it lightly against a rock so that it held firm.

He felt another Yak close by, and knew it was his mother.
She licked him.

"Yaks can't go to the seaside, Yak," she said. "It's much too far away. And you'd get lost."

Mocka was a speck in the distance.

"Perhaps I could follow Mocka," said Yak. "He passes every morning on his way to the sea."

His mother ate some grass.

Yak wandered down the hill. He crossed a mountain stream, stepping on the stones.

"Hello, Yak! Hello, Yak!" called the stream. "Look at me! Look at me! I'm going to the seaside."

Yak stumbled on a stone and fell *splash* into the water.

He didn't mind. It was rather fun being carried along by the stream. He lay on his back and watched the sun rise. Then he shut his eyes. It felt funny moving without seeing where he was going, yet rather nice. So he stayed like that.

When he opened his eyes again, the river, now no longer a stream, was flowing gently. The sun was overhead. A heron was standing in the water. As Yak floated by, it stared after him. It had never seen a yak floating down the river before.

"Well," thought the heron, "he's going to get to the seaside soon." He flapped his wings and flew after Yak, who had turned over and was swimming now.

"Mrmph!" Yak called to the heron – it was difficult making Mrmphing noises in the water. "Mrmphlp gulp – where am I?"

The heron didn't hear him, and flew away. Yak was alone on the wide, wide river.

He could feel the shell on his horn. Waves rippled against him. He felt strangely contented. He lapped the water. It was salty!

"Salt!" thought Yak.

"Sea!" thought Yak. Mocka had told him that the sea was salty. He turned over on his back, again, and drifted.

"Shall I shut my eyes again?" he thought. "Shall I keep them shut and see?"

"How can I see if they're shut? I am a silly Yak!"

Yak sometimes talked to himself like this inside his head.

"I mean," he thought, "see what HAPPENS. It's a sort of 'See what happens' day." So he shut his eyes.

He could hear a boat go 'chug chug chug' as it passed, in the distance.

Yak floated on.

Next time he opened his eyes, the sun was further across the sky and Yak felt hungry. So he paddled towards the shore and climbed the river bank and ate some grass.

There was a strange smell in the air. And a noise.

He'd heard that noise before in his shell.

He stumbled hurriedly through the grass.

He climbed a hill.

There, ahead, was a vast expanse of water.

Yak gazed at it for a long time. All around, the sky and the sea touched, and the waves sparkled in the sunshine.

To his right, on the yellow sand, some children were watching something.

Yak went to look.

It was a Punch and Judy show. Mocka had told him about those. He stayed to watch.

Presently a man with an ice cream cart came by.

"Lovely ice-a-creams!" he called. "Ten-a-pence each!"

The children bought some. Yak went on following the man, who stopped and looked at him. Then he smiled and gave Yak an ice cream.

Lick – "Oh yum!" Yak liked it very much.

They walked on, together. In the distance were some rocks.

"You-a go-a long-a there-a, Yak-a," said the man.

He was an Italian man.

"You go-a long-a there, and find-a nice-a cave-a." He lifted his hat and said goodbye.

"Mrmph!" went Yak, and walked till he came to the rocks. It was quiet there.

Yak did find a cave. A nice dry cave. He rested and looked at the sea.

"I'm at the seaside!" he thought. "Really at the seaside!"

The waves rolled ashore – minute after minute, hour after hour, nearer and nearer, rolling among the pebbles and sand, as Yak lay watching.

A big ship, tiny in the distance, crept, like a snail, across the horizon.

Some seagulls flew about, mewing as they played.

Yak looked, but Mocka wasn't among them.

Presently it began to grow dark.

Then darker and darker.

The moon rose and all was still, save for the sound of the waves breaking on the shore.

Yak listened to his shell, again. It made exactly the same noise as the sea.

What a day it had been! He had come such a long way and seen so many new things.

He listened to his shell just once more. Then curled up so that his warm hair covered his nose and his legs, and soon fell fast asleep.

Jerome, the Lion and the Donkey

Jerome was a holy man who lived in a monastery many hundreds of years ago. One hot afternoon, he and some of the other monks were sitting together, when a lion appeared in the courtyard of the monastery. There was panic and confusion as several of the monks thought the lion had come to kill them, but Jerome saw that one of the lion's paws was swollen and the lion was limping.

"Calm yourselves, brothers," he said, "and bring me some clean cloths and warm water. The poor creature has come to us for help. We need not be afraid of him."

Cautiously they gathered round, and one man fetched warm water, another a clean cloth for a bandage, and another some ointment made from healing herbs. Very gently, and with great care, Jerome knelt by the lion, and first bathed and then bound up the torn foot. The lion had obviously been in great pain but he seemed much better after the treatment and lay down peacefully in the shade of the courtyard and slept.

The next day the lion was still there, and so Jerome bathed his paw again. It looked cleaner and less swollen, and the lion seemed grateful for the help he had received. So it was for several days, until the paw was completely healed.

Most of the monks had overcome their fear of having a lion in the monastery, but nonetheless they were pleased to hear he was cured, as they thought he would now go away.

But the lion did not go. He stayed and followed Jerome when he went to work in the fields, and lay down in the courtyard when Jerome was in the monastery. Several monks felt certain that a fully grown lion, no longer in pain, must be savage, and that sooner or later someone would be hurt. However, when they tried sending the lion away – even when Jerome left him in the woods himself – he always came back to the monastery.

"It's no good," said Jerome. "He has come to stay."

"It is not right that he should stay for he does no work," said one of the monks. "None of us stays here without working."

So Jerome said, "Well, let us think of some work he can do."

Then one old monk whose job it was to take the donkey to the woods every day to collect logs for the fire, said, "Let the lion go with the donkey each day. He will stop wild beasts attacking the donkey better than I can, and I will then be free to do other jobs in the monastery."

So it was agreed, and each day the lion and the donkey set out together for the woods. On the way the donkey would eat grass in the pasture while the lion guarded him. The woodmen would then fill the baskets that were strapped to the donkey's back with logs, and together they would return.

"What a useful member of the community he is," said some of the monks, while others still took care not to get too close in case the lion turned savage.

One day, as the donkey was grazing, the lion found a shady spot to lie and wait for his friend, and in the still of the hot day he dropped off to sleep. As he slept some travelling merchants with a string of camels came by, and saw the donkey grazing alone.

"Look at that," they said to each other. "A donkey is just what we want to lead our camels. No one seems to be looking after it. Let's take it quickly."

Now the merchants, although they could see no one, knew they were stealing, for the donkey had baskets on his back and obviously belonged to someone, but they reckoned they would be over the border into a different country by nightfall, and nobody would ever know where the donkey had gone. They threw the baskets behind a bush, and led him off at the head of their string of camels.

When the lion awoke and found the donkey had disappeared, he roared in misery, and returned that evening to the monastery his head hanging low with shame. The monks crowded round him, some of them saying,

"A wild beast should never be trusted. He has killed and eaten our dear donkey, even after all these months of appearing to be such a gentle animal."

Jerome said, "Do not judge him too quickly, brothers. Let us go to the wood and see if we find something to show us what happened to the donkey."

So a group of monks set off, and when they found the donkey's baskets, they said, "Look, here is the evidence we wanted. This shows the donkey was killed by the savage lion."

But the lion still showed no sign of being fierce, so Jerome suggested to the angry monks that since the lion was obviously at fault, in that he had failed to guard the donkey, he should now do the donkey's work.

"Let him go to the woods each day with the donkey's baskets strapped to his back," he said, "and let him carry the logs we need as the little donkey used to do."

The monks agreed to Jerome's plan, and each morning after that the lion set out for the woods alone, with the donkey's baskets strapped to his back.

A whole year went by, and during this time Jerome was made the head monk in the monastery because his wisdom and his gentleness were respected by all. The lion, still Jerome's friend and companion, continued to go each day to get wood for the monastery. He did the task without complaining, almost as if he were saying, "I am sorry about the donkey," each time they strapped the baskets on him.

One day, when he was padding gently to the woods, he caught sight of his old friend the donkey. The traveling merchants were once more on their old route and the little donkey they had stolen was leading their string of camels. Without hesitating, the lion gave a great roar and bounded over to the donkey. The merchants, thinking they were being attacked by a wild and ferocious lion, fled in terror, while the donkey gave a bray of delight and trotted over to his friend the lion.

Together they set off toward the monastery, for the lion wished to show the monks that he had found the little donkey. For a whole year the camels had followed the donkey, and now they continued to do so. The merchants were all hiding and could do nothing to stop them. So the monks looked up in astonishment to see the strange procession of lion, donkey and camels coming into the courtyard.

"I see," said Jerome, "that the lion has made good his fault. He has found the donkey he so carelessly lost a year ago. We have been harsh to doubt him, and to think he might have killed the donkey."

Just then the courtyard was filled with angry merchants who had followed the camels. Now they asked to speak to the head of the monastery, and Jerome stepped forward.

"You have stolen our donkey, our camels and all our wares," they shouted angrily. "We demand you return them at once."

"We have stolen nothing," Jerome replied quietly. "Your camels and the goods they carry are yours to take away. The camels came here of their own accord. But the donkey is not yours to take. He was ours, and he was stolen last year. It must have been you who took him, and hid his baskets behind the bush. Now he has come back with his friend the lion to his real owners."

The merchants then changed their tone. "We found the donkey on its own one day. We are really very sorry," they told the monks. Promising they would not steal again and still eyeing the lion with fear, they went on their way, taking their camels and goods with them.

The donkey and the lion went out together each day as before, and the monks who had thought the lion a savage beast were sorry that they had misjudged him. The lion lived for many more years in the monastery, and in his old age he would sit at Jerome's feet as the holy man wrote books. The monastery was known far and wide as a place where wisdom and gentleness were always to be found.

The Tinder Box

A soldier was marching along the road on his way home from the wars one day when an old woman came out from behind a tree and stopped him. She was as ugly as a witch but she seemed friendly enough as she admired the soldier's sword.

"How would you like to take home with you as much money as you can carry, soldier?" she asked.

"I'd like it a lot," he said, "only where I can find the money, old woman?"

"Listen and I'll tell you," the witch woman replied. "If you climb into this tree, you will find it is hollow. Go down inside it and you will find yourself in a shaft going deep down into the earth. At the bottom there is a passage and you will see three doors.

"The first door leads to a room guarded by a fierce dog with eyes as big as tea cups. In it you will find as much bronze money as you could want. Take this apron of mine and spread it out on the floor. If the dog sits on it he will do you no harm. But if you prefer it, go on to the second door."

"What shall I find there?" interrupted the soldier.

"Ah!" said the old woman. "There you will find as much silver as you can carry, and more. But this room is guarded by a dog whose eyes are as big as mill wheels. He too is fierce, but will not hurt you once he has sat on my apron."

"In the last room you will find gold coins, masses and masses of gold coins, but take care here, for the dog that guards the gold has eyes as big as towers. He is even fiercer, but he too will not hurt you if he sits on my apron."

"It all sounds very good, old woman," said the soldier cheerfully, "but what are you going to get out of it? I can't believe you would give me this chance to get rich without wanting a favour of some kind yourself."

"Quite right, soldier," she replied. "You must bring me the tinder box that lies on the table at the end of the passage. My grandmother gave it to me, but I forgot to bring it up last time I was down there. I'm too old now to climb down the shaft to fetch it. Tie this rope round your waist so that I can help pull you up when you have finished."

The soldier tied the rope round his waist and climbed into the hollow tree. It was just as the old woman had described and the soldier clambered down a long shaft deep into the ground, and found himself in a passage. It was lit by many candles so he could see the three doors quite clearly.

He opened the first door and gasped with pleasure and fright. There before him were chests and chests of bronze money but standing in front of them was a fierce-looking dog with eyes as big as tea cups. The soldier whistled cheerfully and laid the witch's apron on the floor.

To his relief the dog sat on the apron and the soldier went over to the chests and stuffed his pockets with the bronze money. Then he persuaded the dog to move, picked up the apron and returned to the passage.

The soldier went on to the second door, and when he peeped inside he could not believe his eyes. There was the fiercest-looking dog he had ever seen with eyes so huge they looked as big as mill wheels, and behind him were caskets full of silver. The greedy soldier put the witch's apron on the ground and as soon as the dog was sitting on it, he emptied all the bronze money out of his pockets, picked up handfuls of silver coins and filled his pockets and his knapsack. He was so weighed down when he left the room he could scarcely pick up the witch's apron. He then staggered on down the passage to the third door.

Inside, the whole room seemed to sparkle from the gold the soldier could see, but between him and the gold stood the most ferocious dog imaginable. The dog was huge and his eyes as they stared at the soldier were as big as towers. The soldier spread the apron on the floor very carefully and to his relief the dog sat on it and became quite friendly. The soldier quickly threw all the silver he had collected down on the floor, and picked up gold coins as fast as he could, cramming them into his pockets, his knapsack and even his hat.

The soldier went back to the shaft to climb up into the hollow tree. He tugged at the rope so the old woman could help him, but she called down, "Did you get my tinder box, soldier?"

"Why no, I forgot!" called back the soldier. "I'll get it now."

He went back along the passage and found the tinder box where she had said it would be, and he picked it up and returned to the bottom of the shaft.

As soon as he was out of the hollow tree the soldier asked the old woman why the tinder box was so important to her but she would not tell him. "If you don't answer me," he shouted, "I shall cut off your head with my fine sword," but the old woman just held out her hand for the tinder box. The soldier, who was used to getting his own way, drew his sword and with one swift stroke he chopped off her head.

The soldier went on his way cheerfully, and in the evening he came to a big town and took rooms in the best inn. The innkeeper was surprised that a mere soldier wanted such an expensive room, and the boot boy wondered at the shabby old boots put out to be cleaned, but they said nothing, for they had seen the gleam of gold in the soldier's hand.

The next day, the soldier went out and bought himself fine clothes and new boots. For many months he stayed on in the inn, and lived like a rich gentleman. He made a lot of friends, gave many parties and enjoyed himself tremendously. Each day his supply of gold got less as he spent money but never earned any, until the day came when he had nothing left at all.

Now the soldier had to move into a small dismal attic room where he was cold and hungry. His friends did not come and see him any more, indeed they seemed to have forgotten all about him. One dark night as he sat huddled in a chair trying to keep warm, he caught sight of an old candle stub which he thought might give him a few moments of warmth and light. Remembering the old woman's tinder box, he struck it once to light the candle. To his amazement he saw the dog with eyes as big as tea cups in the room with him.

"What do you want, master?" the dog asked. "Shall I fetch you some money?" and even as the soldier nodded the dog disappeared and returned with a bag of bronze coins in his mouth.

The soldier struck the tinder box twice and the dog with eyes as big as mill wheels was there, saying, "What do you want, master?", and he too disappeared and came back with a bag of money, but this time it was in silver coins. The soldier struck the tinder box again three times, and there was the huge dog with eyes as big as towers. In a flash, he too disappeared and returned with a bag of gold coins.

"Now I know why the old woman was so anxious to get this tinder box," said the soldier, smiling to himself.

He moved the next day into expensive lodgings and all his friends came to see him again, and the parties started once more. The soldier seemed to have everything he could want, but there was one thing he could not do, and this annoyed him very much. At the end of the town was the king's palace, and it was said the king had a most beautiful daughter. The soldier longed to see her but his friends told him it was impossible.

"No one is allowed to see her," they said. "The king was once told that she would marry a common soldier so now he keeps her guarded in the palace where she will never meet anyone but a prince."

The soldier often thought about the princess and wondered how he could arrange to see her. One night he had an idea. He struck the tinder box once and when the dog with eyes as big as tea cups appeared and asked, "What can I do for you, master?" he did not ask for money as he usually did, but told the dog he wished to see the princess. In no time at all the dog returned carrying the sleeping princess on its back. The soldier found her extremely beautiful and made up his mind that each night one of the dogs should bring the princess to him.

One morning the princess told her parents of a dream she often had. "It is such a strange dream," she said. "A huge dog with enormous eyes appears and carries me into the town and then to a room where there is a fine rich gentleman."

The king and queen were worried and asked one of the ladies-in-waiting to watch the princess during the night. The first evening that she was watching, the lady-in-waiting saw a great dog with eyes as big as mill wheels come and take the princess away on its back. She followed them through the town to the house where the dog took the princess, and then she made a cross on the door with chalk. But the dog saw her and, after he had returned the princess to the palace, he put chalk crosses on all the doors in the town.

The next day the king and queen, led by the lady-in-waiting, set out to find the scoundrel who sent his dog each night to fetch their daughter, but as they found each door marked with a cross they were completely confused. The queen was determined to find out what happened to their daughter each night, so she made another plan. She filled a little silk bag with fine flour, snipped a small hole in the corner and tied this to her daughter before she went to bed.

64

The next morning she and the king were able to follow the trail of flour to the soldier's lodgings. Immediately the king had the soldier thrown into prison, and announced that he would be executed the next day.

As the soldier sat in his cell waiting for death, a boy outside tripped and lost his shoe through the cell grating. "If you want it back," called the soldier, "go to my lodgings and bring me my tinder box. I'll give you four pence too." The boy went willingly to fetch the tinder box for he was glad to earn four pence.

A large crowd gathered to see the soldier executed. As he climbed the scaffold the soldier asked for one last wish.

"Let me smoke my pipe one last time before I die," he said. It seemed a reasonable request, and so it was granted. The soldier filled his pipe and took out his tinder box. He struck it once, then twice, then three times. The three huge dogs appeared and asked their master what he wanted. He shouted, "Save me!"

The dogs bounded forward and the king and queen and all the guards were slain. Most of the crowd ran away, but those who stayed decided that the soldier should be their new king. They could see he was very powerful!

The soldier gladly accepted and the first thing he did was to marry the beautiful princess. They lived together in the palace and the soldier always had everything he wanted, for the dog with eyes as big as tea cups, the dog with eyes as big as mill wheels and the dog with eyes as big as towers were always there to carry out his orders. And you can be certain that, for the rest of his life, he was always careful to carry the tinder box with him wherever he went.

Country Mouse and Town Mouse

There was once a little mouse who lived very happily in the country. He ate grains of wheat and grass seeds, nibbled turnips in the fields, and had a safe snug house in a hedgerow. On sunny days he would curl up on the bank near his nest and warm himself, and in the winter he would scamper in the fields with his friends.

He was delighted when he heard his cousin from the town was coming to visit him, and fetched some of the best food from his store cupboard so he could share it with him. When his cousin arrived, he proudly offered him some fine grains of dried wheat and some particularly good nuts he had put away in the fall.

His cousin, the town mouse, however, was not impressed. "You call this good food?" he asked. "My dear fellow, you must come and stay with me in the city. I will then show you what fine living is all about. Come with me tomorrow, for not a day should be wasted before you see what excellent hospitality I can offer you."

So the two mice traveled up to town. From his cousin's mousehole, the country mouse watched with wonder a grand dinner which the people who lived in the house were giving. He stared in amazement at the variety of cheese, the beautiful vegetables, the fresh white rolls, the fruit, and the wine served from glittering decanters.

"Now's our chance," said the town mouse, as the dining-room emptied. The two mice came out of the hole, and scurried across the floor to where the crumbs lay scattered beneath the table. Never had the country mouse eaten such delicacies, or tasted such fine food. "My cousin was right," he thought as he nibbled at a fine juicy grape. "This is the good life!"

All of a sudden a great fierce furry beast leapt into the room and pounced on the mice.

"Run for it, little cousin!" shouted the town mouse, and together they reached the mousehole gasping for breath and shaking with fright. The cat settled down outside the hole, tail twitching, to wait for them.

"Don't worry. He will get bored soon, and go and amuse himself elsewhere. We can then go and finish our feast," said the town mouse.

"You can go out there again, if you like," said the country mouse. "I shall not. I am leaving tonight by the back door to return to my country home. I would rather gnaw a humble vegetable there than live here amidst these dangers."

So the country mouse lived happily in the country, the town mouse in the town. Each was content with the way of life he was used to, and had no desire to change.

Elephant and Rabbit

Elephant and Rabbit were good friends. One day they were hungry so they went to a farmer and asked him if they could work in his fields in return for some food.

"Of course," said the farmer, "but you must promise to work hard."

"Oh yes," said Rabbit eagerly. Elephant just made a grunting sound.

The farmer saw they were really hungry so he showed them what he wanted done in his fields and then he put some beans on to cook so they would be ready to eat when the work was finished. Rabbit worked hard, while Elephant did very little. He said he was too hot or that his foot was sore, and by the time Rabbit had finished his share of the work, Elephant had barely started.

"Oh dear!" thought Rabbit, "I must help Elephant or we will never get that food."

So Rabbit started on Elephant's share of the work, and still Elephant did very little. At last the work was finished.

"Now we can eat," said Rabbit, and he went over to where the beans were bubbling and boiling in the pot.

"Wait a minute," said Elephant. "I am so dirty from all that work, I must go down to the river and wash before we eat."

Now you may not know it, but elephants in those days could take off their skins. They had sixteen buttons down the front, and when these were undone an elephant could step out of its skin. The elephant in this story went down to the river, and undid the sixteen buttons down his front, pop, pop, pop. He stepped out of his skin, folded it up and hid it under a bush. Then he rushed towards Rabbit making a tremendous roaring noise as he went. Rabbit, as you can imagine, was scared out of his wits. He ran away as fast as he could, and hid.

Elephant quickly gobbled up all the beans that were bubbling and boiling in the pot. Then he went back to the river bank to pick up his skin. He stepped back into it, did up the sixteen buttons, and sauntered back to where the beanpot was now lying empty. There was Rabbit, waiting for him.

"Now," said Elephant, "at last we can eat."

"Oh dear no," said Rabbit in tears. "While you were down by the river washing, a great monster came roaring up. I was so scared I ran away and while I was gone the monster ate up all the beans. I am afraid we shall go to bed hungry tonight." Rabbit was so flustered that he did not notice that Elephant was not particularly hungry.

The next day much the same thing happened. Rabbit worked hard all day while Elephant made one excuse after another for doing very little. In the evening Elephant once more went down to the river to wash before they ate the beans the farmer had cooked for them.

Pop, pop, pop, Elephant undid his sixteen buttons, stepped out of his skin, and rushed up again, frightening Rabbit out of his wits for the second time.

He gobbled down the beans and, when he returned in his skin, he pretended to be very cross that the monster had eaten their food again.

Rabbit, meanwhile, had begun to wonder what an elephant would look like without his skin. He knew an elephant had sixteen buttons down the front that could be undone and began to think that an elephant without its skin might look rather like the monster who had frightened him when Elephant had been down by the river. So that night before going to sleep Rabbit made a bow and arrow and hid them in the bushes.

All the next day Rabbit worked hard in the farmer's fields while Elephant made excuses. He said the stony ground hurt his feet, the flies were troubling him and the sun was too hot. These and many other things prevented him from working all day. By evening Rabbit was really hungry, and determined to eat those bubbling boiling beans himself. This time, when Elephant said he must go down to the river to wash before their meal, Rabbit took up his bow and arrow.

Pop, pop, pop, Elephant undid his buttons, stepped out of his skin and rushed into the clearing where Rabbit was waiting. *Ping!* An arrow flew from Rabbit's bow, and struck Elephant on the shoulder. If he had been wearing his skin he would hardly have noticed, but without his skin, it really hurt!

"Ow! Ow! Ow!" shrieked Elephant, forgetting he was a monster, but he got no sympathy from Rabbit.

"Go back and get into your skin, you wicked elephant," said Rabbit, "and stop making such a fuss. The arrow did not hurt that much."

When Elephant came back in his skin he found Rabbit had eaten all those bubbling boiling beans. It was his turn now to go to bed hungry and the next day Rabbit made a new arrangement with the farmer. Elephant had to look for food elsewhere and, as far as I know, he never took off his skin again.

Next time you see an elephant look carefully and you will see his skin is all loose and full of folds and creases, and looks as though it could be taken off. But over the years the sixteen buttons and buttonholes must have disappeared for, however hard you look, I don't think you will ever see them.

The Fox and the Crow

A crow was sitting on the branch of a tree one day, with a large piece of cheese in his mouth. A fox caught the scent of the cheese and, following his nose, found himself at the foot of the tree where the crow sat. The cheese looked and smelt so delicious that it made the fox's mouth water and he longed to eat it. The cheese, however, was well out of his reach, and the fox knew only too well that the crow would not drop it without some good reason. The fox thought a little, and decided to talk to the crow:

"Good day Mr Crow! How fine you look sitting there. How glossy and black your feathers are. But tell me, is your voice as fine as your plumage? If it is, you would be proclaimed by all to be the most splendid creature in the whole wood!"

The crow was greatly impressed by the fox's words. He was proud that the fox admired his sleek black feathers and gleaming beak and eyes, so he decided to show off his fine voice too. The fox would then see that indeed he was the most splendid creature in the whole wood.

He opened his beak wide to sing and, as he did so, the cheese fell to the ground. In a flash the fox snatched it up and from a safe distance he said:

"My dear Sir, you should know that flattery gets nowhere unless those who hear it believe it. This lesson, as you can see, has cost you a fine piece of cheese."
The crow realized he had been foolish, and vowed, a little too late, that he would never be tricked the same way again.

The Baker's Cat

Joan Aiken

Once there was an old lady, Mrs Jones, who lived with her cat, Mog. Mrs Jones kept a baker's shop, in a little tiny town, at the bottom of a valley between two mountains.

Every morning you could see Mrs Jones's light twinkle on, long before all the other houses in the town, because she got up very early to bake loaves and buns and jam tarts and Welsh cakes.

First thing in the morning Mrs Jones lit a big fire. Then she made dough, out of flour and water and sugar and yeast. Then she put the dough into pans and set it in front of the fire to rise.

Mog got up early too. He got up to catch mice. When he had chased all the mice out of the bakery, he wanted to sit in front of the warm fire. But Mrs Jones wouldn't let him, because of the loaves and buns there, rising in their pans.

She said, "Don't sit on the buns, Mog."

The buns were rising nicely. They were getting fine and big. That is what yeast does. It makes bread and buns and cakes swell up and get bigger and bigger.

As Mog was not allowed to sit by the fire, he went to play in the sink.

Most cats hate water, but Mog didn't. He loved it. He liked to sit by the tap, hitting the drops with his paw as they fell, and getting water all over his whiskers!

75

What did Mog look like? His back, and his sides, and his legs down as far as where his socks would have come to, and his face and ears and his tail were all marmalade colored. His stomach and his waistcoat and his paws were white. And he had a white tassel at the tip of his tail, white fringes to his ears, and white whiskers. The water made his marmalade fur go almost fox color and his paws and waistcoat shining-white clean.

But Mrs Jones said, "Mog, you are getting too excited. You are shaking water all over my pans of buns, just when they are getting nice and big. Run along and play outside."

Mog was affronted. He put his ears and tail down (when cats are pleased they put their ears and tails up) and he went out. It was raining hard.

A rushing rocky river ran through the middle of the town. Mog went and sat in the water and looked for fish. But there were no fish in that part of the river. Mog got wetter and wetter. But he didn't care. Presently he began to sneeze.

Then Mrs Jones opened her door and called, "Mog! I have put the buns in the oven. You can come in now, and sit by the fire."

Mog was so wet that he was shiny all over, as if he had been polished. As he sat by the fire he sneezed nine times.

Mrs. Jones said, "Oh dear, Mog, are you catching a cold?"

She dried him with a towel and gave him some warm milk with yeast in it. Yeast is good for people when they are poorly.

Then she left him sitting in front of the fire and began making jam tarts. When she had put the tarts in the oven she went out shopping, taking her umbrella.

But what do you think was happening to Mog?

The yeast was making him rise.

As he sat dozing in front of the lovely warm fire he was growing bigger and bigger.

First he grew as big as a sheep.

Then he grew as big as a donkey.

Then he grew as big as a cart-horse.

Then he grew as big as a hippopotamus.

By now he was too big for Mrs Jones's little kitchen, but he was far too big to get through the door. He just burst the walls.

When Mrs Jones came home with her shopping-bag and her umbrella she cried out,

"Mercy me, what is happening to my house?"

The whole house was bulging. It was swaying. Huge whiskers were poking out of the kitchen window. A marmalade-colored paw came out of one bedroom window, and an ear with a white fringe out of the other.

"Morow?" said Mog. He was waking up from his nap and trying to stretch.

Then the whole house fell down.

"Oh, Mog!" cried Mrs Jones. "Look what you've done."

The people in the town were very astonished when they saw what had happened.

They gave Mrs Jones the Town Hall to live in, because they were so fond of her (and her buns). But they were not so sure about Mog.

The Mayor said, "Suppose he goes on growing and breaks our Town Hall? Suppose he turns fierce? It would not be safe to have him in the town, he is too big."

Mrs Jones said, "Mog is a gentle cat. He would not hurt anybody."

"We will wait and see about that," said the Mayor. "Suppose he sat down on someone? Suppose he was hungry? What will he eat? He had better live outside the town, up on the mountain."

So everybody shouted, "Shoo! Scram! Pssst! Shoo!" and poor Mog was driven outside the town gates. It was still raining hard. Water was rushing down the mountains. Not that Mog cared.

But poor Mrs Jones was very sad. She began making a new lot of loaves and buns in the Town Hall, crying into them so much that the dough was too wet, and very salty.

Mog walked up the valley between the two mountains. By now he was bigger than an elephant – almost as big as a whale! When the sheep on the mountain saw him coming, they were scared to death and galloped away. But he took no notice of them. He was looking for fish in the river. He caught lots of fish! He was having a fine time.

By now it had been raining for so long that Mog heard a loud, watery roar at the top of the valley. He saw a huge wall of water coming towards him. The river was beginning to flood, as more and more rain-water poured down into it, off the mountains.

Mog thought, "If I don't stop that water, all these fine fish will be washed away."

So he sat down, plump in the middle of the valley, and he spread himself out like a big, fat cottage loaf.

The water could not get by.

The people in the town had heard the roar of the flood-water. They were very frightened. The Mayor shouted, "Run up the mountains before the water gets to the town, or we shall all be drowned!"

So they all rushed up the mountains, some on one side of the town, some on the other.

What did they see then?

Why, Mog, sitting in the middle of the valley. Beyond him was a great lake.

"Mrs Jones," said the Mayor, "can you make your cat stay there till we have built a dam across the valley, to keep all that water back?"

"I will try," said Mrs Jones. "He mostly sits still if he is tickled under his chin."

So for three days everybody in the town took turns tickling Mog under his chin with hay-rakes. He purred and purred and purred. His purring made big waves roll right across the lake of flood-water.

All this time the best builders were making a great dam across the valley.

People brought Mog all sorts of nice things to eat, too – bowls of cream and condensed milk, liver and bacon, sardines, even chocolate! But he was not very hungry. He had eaten so much fish.

On the third day they finished the dam. The town was safe.

The Mayor said, "I can see now that Mog is a gentle cat. He can live in the Town Hall with you, Mrs Jones. Here is a badge for him to wear."

The badge was on a silver chain to go round his neck. It said MOG SAVED OUR TOWN.

So Mrs Jones and Mog lived happily ever after in the Town Hall. If you should go to the little town of Carnmog you may see the policeman holding up the traffic while Mog walks through the streets on his way to catch fish in the lake for breakfast. His tail waves above the houses and his whiskers rattle against the upstairs windows. But people know he will not hurt them, because he is a gentle cat.

He loves to play in the lake and sometimes he gets so wet that he sneezes. But Mrs Jones is not going to give him any more yeast.

He is quite big enough already!

Henny Penny

One day Henny Penny was scratching in the farmyard looking for something good to eat when, suddenly, something hit her on the head.

"My goodness me!" she said. "The sky must be falling down. I must go and tell the king."

She had not gone far when she met her friend Cocky Locky.

"Where are you going in such a hurry?" he called out.

"I am going to tell the king that the sky is falling down," said Henny Penny.

"I will come with you," said Cocky Locky.

So Henny Penny and Cocky Locky hurried along together towards the king's palace. On the way they saw Ducky Lucky swimming on the pond. "Where are you going?" he called out.

"We are going to tell the king the sky is falling down," replied Henny Penny. "We must go quickly, as there is no time to lose."

"I will come with you," said Ducky Lucky, shaking the water off his feathers.

So Henny Penny, Cocky Locky and Ducky Lucky hurried on together towards the king's palace. On the way they met Goosey Loosey, who called out, "Where are you all going in such a hurry?"

"We are on our way to tell the king the sky is falling down," said Henny Penny.

"I will come with you," said Goosey Loosey.

So Henny Penny, Cocky Locky, Ducky Lucky and Goosey Loosey hurried on together towards the king's palace.

Round the next corner they met Turkey Lurkey. "Where are you all going on this fine day?" she called out to them.

"It won't be a fine day for long," replied Henny Penny. "The sky is falling down, and we are hurrying to tell the king."

"I will come with you," said Turkey Lurkey.

So Henny Penny, Cocky Locky, Ducky Lucky, Goosey Loosey and Turkey Lurkey all went on towards the king's palace.

Now on their way they met Foxy Loxy who asked, "Where are you going in such a hurry?"

"We are going to the king's palace to tell him the sky is falling down," replied Henny Penny.

"That is a very important message," said Foxy Loxy. "I will come with you. In fact if you follow me I can show you a short cut to the king's palace, so you will get there sooner.

So Henny Penny, Cocky Locky, Ducky Lucky, Goosey Loosey and Turkey Lurkey all followed Foxy Loxy. He led them to the wood, and up to a dark hole, which was the door to his home. Inside his wife and five hungry children were waiting for him to bring home some dinner.

That, I am sorry to say, was the end of Cocky Locky, Ducky Lucky, Goosey Loosey and Turkey Lurkey, for one by one they all followed Foxy Loxy into his home, and they were all eaten up by the hungry fox family.

Henny Penny was the last to enter the Fox's hole and she heard Cocky Locky crowing in alarm in front of her. Squawking with fright and scattering feathers, she turned and ran as fast as she could for the safety of her own farmyard. There she stayed and she never did tell the king that the sky was falling down.

The Fisherman's Son

A long time ago, when impossible things were possible, there was a fisherman and his son. One day when the fisherman hauled in his net he found a huge gleaming red fish among the rest of his catch. For a few moments he was so excited he could only stare at it. "This fish will make me famous," he thought. " Never before has a fisherman caught such a fish."

"Stay here," he said to his son, "and look after these fish, while I go and fetch the cart to take them home."

The fisherman's son, too, was excited by the great red fish, and while he was waiting for his father, he stroked it and started to talk to it.

"It seems a shame that a beautiful creature like you should not swim free," he said, and no sooner had he spoken than he decided to put the fish back into the sea. The great red fish slipped gratefully into the water, raised its head and spoke to the boy.

"It was kind of you to save my life. Take this bone which I have pulled from my fin. If ever you need my help, hold it up, call me, and I will come at once."

The fisherman's son placed the bone carefully in his pocket just as his father reappeared with the cart. When the father saw that his son had let the great red fish go he was angry beyond belief.

"Get out of my sight," he shouted at his son, "and never let me set eyes on you again."

The boy went off sadly. He did not know where to go or what to do. In time he found himself in a great forest. He walked on and on, till suddenly he was startled by a stag rushing through the trees towards him. It was being chased by a pack of ferocious hounds followed by hunters, and it was clearly exhausted and could run no further. The boy felt sorry for the stag and took hold of its antlers as the hounds and then the hunters appeared.

"Shame on you," he said, "for chasing a tame stag. Go and find a wild beast to hunt for your sport."

The hunters, seeing the stag standing quietly by the boy thought it must be a pet and so they turned and rode off to another part of the forest.

"It was most kind of you to save my life," said the stag, and it pulled a fine brown hair from its coat. "Take this and if ever you need help, hold it out and call me. I will come at once."

The fisherman's son put the hair in his pocket with the fishbone. He thanked the stag which disappeared among the trees and wandered on once more.

As he walked he heard a strange fluttering sound overhead and, looking up, he saw a great bird – a crane – being attacked by an eagle. The crane was weak and could fight no more, and the eagle was about to kill it. The kindhearted boy picked up a stick and threw it at the eagle, which flew off at once, fearful of this new enemy. The crane sank to the ground.

As he ran he kept muttering, "Opposite, ottipis, ossipit" and he got all mixed up. So that when he got back to the other animals all he could say was, "Well, Jemma did tell me the name but I can't remember whether it's ossipit, ottipis, or ossupit. I do know it's got something to do with 'opposite'."

"Oh dear," they all sighed. "We had better send someone with a better memory."

"I'll go," said the goat. "I never forget anything." So he headed straight for Jemma's hut, grunting and snorting all the way.

"I'm sorry to bother you again, Mrs Jemma," he panted, "but that stupid hare couldn't remember the name of the tree. Do you mind telling it me once more?"

"Gladly I will," replied the old woman. "It's ossopit. Just think of 'opposite' and then sort of say it backwards:

opposite – ossopit."

"Rightee-oh," said the goat, "and thank you very much, I'm sure."

And off he galloped, fast as he could, kicking up clouds of dust, and all the way he kept saying:

"Ottopis, oppossit, possitto, otto . . ." until he got back.

"I know the name of that tree," he said. "It's oppitis, n . . . no . . . ossipit, n . . . no . . . otup . . . oh dear. . . I just can't get it right."

"Well, who can we send this time?" they all asked. They didn't want to bother old Jemma again.

"I'm perfectly willing to have a go," piped up a young sparrow. "I'll be back in no time," and with a whisk of his tail he had flown off before anyone could stop him.

"Good morrow, gentle Jemma," he said. "Could you please tell me the name of that tree just *once* more. Hare and goat could *not* get it right."

"Right gladly I will," said old Jemma patiently. "It's ossopit, oss-o-pit. It's a wee bit difficult but just think of 'opposite' and then sort of say it backwards:

opposite – ossopit."

"I'm most grateful, madam," said the sparrow and flew off twittering to himself: "Opposite, ossitup, ottupus, oissopit," until he finally got back to his famishing friends.

"Do tell us, sparrow," they all cried.

"Yes," chirped the sparrow. "It's definitely 'ossitup', n . . . no . . . oittuisip, n . . . no . . . oippisuit . . . Oh dear, I give up. So very sorry."

By now the animals were desperate. Just imagine them all sitting round the gorgeous tree and unable to pick any of its mouth-watering fruit.

Suddenly up spoke the tortoise. "I shall go," he said. "I know it will take a bit of time but I will not forget the name once I've been told. My family has the finest reputation in the world for good memories."

"No," they moaned. "You are too slow. We shall all be dead by the time you get back."

"Why not let me take tortoise on my back?" asked the zebra. "I'm hopeless at remembering things but my speed is second to none. I'll have him back here in no time at all." They all thought this was a splendid idea and so off raced the zebra with the tortoise clinging to his back.

"Good morning, Madam Jemma," said the tortoise. "I'm sorry I have no time to alight. But if we don't get the name of that tree most of us will be dead by tonight. That's why I've come on zebra's back. He's a bit faster than I am, you know."

"Yes, I rather think he is," smiled old Jemma benignly.

"Well, it's OSSOPIT. Just think of 'opposite' and then sort of say it backwards, like this: opposite – oss-o-pit."

"Just let me repeat it three times before I go," said the tortoise, "Just to see if I get it right." And then he said it, very, very slowly, deliberately and loudly, and nodding his tiny head at each syllable:

"OSS-O-PIT, OSS-O-PIT, OSS-O-PIT."

"Bravo!" said Jemma, "you'll never forget it now."

And she was right.

The zebra thudded back hot foot and the tortoise was never in any doubt that he had the name right at last.

"It's OSS-O-PIT," he announced to his ravenous friends.

"Ossopit, ossopit, ossopit," they all cried. "It's an ossopit tree, and it's perfectly safe to eat." And they all helped themselves to the wonderful fruit. You just can't imagine how delicious it tasted.

And to show how grateful they were, they appointed the tortoise their Chief Adviser on Important Matters (he has C.A.I.M. after his name). And he still is Chief Adviser to this very day.

The Lion and the Mouse

A lion was lying asleep one day when a little mouse scampered over him, and woke him up. The lion put out his great big paw and trapped the mouse. He was just going to kill him when the mouse squeaked,

"I meant you no harm, Lion, please let me go free. If you do I promise I will help you one day."

"How can a mouse ever help a lion?" asked the lion scornfully. But he let the little mouse go, and went back to sleep.

Some time later the lion was caught in a cruel trap laid by some hunters. As he struggled, the ropes tightened around him and eventually he lay on the ground exhausted and gasping for breath. He knew that the hunters would soon come back and kill him.

Suddenly there was a rustling and the little mouse was beside him gnawing at the ropes. Strand by strand they broke as the mouse's sharp teeth worked away, and long before the hunters came back the lion was free.

"You never believed I could help you," said the mouse, "but even a mouse can help a lion, and one good turn deserves another."

The Dragon and the Monkey

Far away in the China Seas lived a dragon and his wife. She was fretful and rather difficult, but he was a kind and loving dragon. As they swam in the warm seas together she was forever complaining and asking her husband to fetch her different foods. He always thought, "This time I will really make her happy, and then how easy and lovely life will be." Yet somehow, whatever delicacy he fetched her, she was never satisfied and always wanted something else.

One day she twitched her tail more than usual, and told her husband that she was not feeling well and that she had heard a monkey's heart was the only thing to cure her.

"You are certainly looking pale, my love," said the dragon, "and you know I would do anything for you, but how can I possibly find you a monkey's heart? Monkeys live up trees, and I could never catch one."

"Now I know you don't love me," cried his wife. "If you did you would find a way to catch one. Now I shall surely die!"

The dragon sighed and swam off across the seas to an island where he knew some monkeys lived. "Somehow," he thought desperately, "I must trick a monkey into coming with me, for I cannot let my wife die."

When he reached the island, he saw a little monkey sitting in a tree. The dragon called out,

"Hello, monkey! It's good to see you! Come down and talk to me. That tree looks so unsafe, you might fall out!"

At that the monkey roared with laughter. "Ha! Ha! Ha! You are funny, dragon. Whoever heard of a monkey falling out of a tree?"

The dragon thought of his wife and tried again.

"I'll show you a tree covered with delicious juicy fruit, monkey. It grows on the other side of the sea."

Again the monkey laughed. "Ha! Ha! Ha! Whoever heard of a monkey swimming across the sea, dragon?"

"I could take you on my back, little Monkey," said the dragon.

The monkey liked this idea and swung out of the tree on to the dragon's back. As he swam across the sea, the dragon thought there was no way the monkey could escape, so he said,

"I could take you on my back, little monkey," said the dragon. trees with delicious fruit where we are going. I am taking you to my wife who wishes to eat your heart. She says it is the only thing that will cure her of her illness."

The monkey looked at the water all around him and saw no way to escape, but he thought quickly, and said,

"Your poor wife! I am sorry to hear she's not well. There is nothing I'd like more than to give her my heart. But what a pity you did not tell me before we left. You obviously did not know, dragon, that we monkeys never carry our hearts with us. I left it behind in the tree where you found me. If you would be kind enough to swim back there with me, I shall willingly fetch it."

So the dragon turned round and swam back to the place where he had found the monkey. With one leap the monkey was in the branches of the tree, safe out of the dragon's reach.

"I'm sorry to disappoint you, dragon," he called out, "but I had my heart with me all the time. You won't trick me out of this tree again. Ha! Ha! Ha!"

There was no way the dragon could reach him and whether or not he ever caught another monkey I do not know. Perhaps he is still looking while his wife swims alone in the China Seas.

Brer Rabbit Gets Himself a House

Long ago an old man called Uncle Remus used to tell stories to a little boy. The two of them lived on a plantation in the south, and the stories were always about certain animals, Brer Rabbit and Brer Fox in particular, but several others too, Brer Bear and Brer Possum for instance. All too often Brer Rabbit, who was an impudent scoundrel, came out best, although he was one of the smallest creatures. Of course, to do this he had to use his wits.

One evening, Uncle Remus ate his supper as usual and then looked at the child over his spectacles and said,

"Now then, honey, I'll just rustle around with my memories and see if I can call to mind how old Brer Rabbit got himself a two-story house without paying much for it."

He paused a moment then he began,

"It turned out one time that a whole lot of creatures decided to build a house together. Old Brer Bear he was among them, and Brer Fox and Brer Wolf and Brer Coon and Brer Possum, and possibly Brer Mink too. Anyway, there was a whole bunch of them, and they set to work and built a house in less than no time. Brer Rabbit, he pretended it made his head swim to climb the scaffolding, and that it made him feel dizzy to work in the sun, but he got a board, and he stuck a pencil behind his ear, and he went around measuring and marking, measuring and marking.

He looked so busy that all the other creatures were sure he was doing the most work, and folks going along the road said, 'My, my, that Brer Rabbit is doing more work than the whole lot of them put together.' Yet all the time Brer Rabbit was doing nothing, and he had plenty of time to lie in the shade scratching fleas off himself.

Meanwhile, the other creatures, they built the house, and it sure was a fine one. It had an upstairs and a downstairs, and chimneys all round, and it had rooms for all the creatures who had helped to make it.

Brer Rabbit, he picked out one of the upstairs rooms, and he got a gun and a brass cannon, and when no one was looking he put them up in the room. Then he got a big bowl of dirty water and carried it up there when no one was looking.

When the house was finished and all the animals were sitting in the parlor after supper, Brer Rabbit, he got up and stretched himself, and made excuses, saying he believed he'd go to his room. When he got there, and while all the others were laughing and chatting and being sociable downstairs, Brer Rabbit stuck his head out of the room and hollered:

'When a big man wants to sit down, whereabouts is he going to sit?' says he.

The other creatures laughed, and called back, 'If a big man like you can't sit in a chair, he'd better sit on the floor.'

'Watch out, down there,' says old Brer Rabbit, 'because I'm going to sit down,' says he.

With that, *bang!* went Brer Rabbit's gun. The other creatures looked round at one another in astonishment as much as to say, 'What in the name of gracious is that?'

They listened and listened, but they didn't hear any more fuss and it wasn't long before they were all chatting and talking again.

Then Brer Rabbit stuck his head out of his room again, and hollered, 'When a big man like me wants to sneeze, whereabouts is he going to sneeze?'

The other creatures called back, 'A big man like you can sneeze anywhere he wants.'

'Watch out down there, then,' says Brer Rabbit, 'because I'm going to sneeze right here,' says he.

With that Brer Rabbit let off his cannon – *bulder-um-m-m!* The window panes rattled. The whole house shook as though it would come down, and old Brer Bear fell out of his rocking chair – *kerblump!*

When they all settled down again Brer Possum and Brer Mink suggested that as Brer Rabbit had such a bad cold they would step outside and get some fresh air. The other creatures said that they would stick it out, and before long they all got their hair smoothed down and began to talk again.

After a while, when they were beginning to enjoy themselves once more, Brer Rabbit hollered out:

'When a big man like me chews tobacco, where is he going to spit?'

The other creatures called back as though they were getting pretty angry:

'Big man or little man, spit where you please!'

Then Brer Rabbit called out, 'This is the way a big man spits,' and with that he tipped over the bowl of dirty water, and when the other creatures heard it coming sloshing down the stairs, my, how they rushed out of the house! Some went out the back door, some went out the front door, some fell out of the windows, some went one way and some another way; but they all got out as quickly as they could.

Then Brer Rabbit, he shut up the house, and fastened the windows and went to bed. He pulled the covers up around his ears, and he slept like a man who doesn't owe anybody anything.

And neither did he owe them," said Uncle Remus to the little boy, "for if the other creatures got scared and ran off from their own house, what business is that of Brer Rabbit? That's what I'd like to know."

Puss-in-Boots

A miller once died, leaving his three sons all that he possessed – his mill, his donkey and his cat. They quickly arranged between them that the eldest son should keep the mill, the middle son the donkey, while the youngest should take the cat.

"It is very hard on me," grumbled the youngest son. "My brothers can earn their living with the mill and the donkey, whereas after I have eaten the cat, I will have nothing."

"Don't talk like that, master," said the cat. "Give me some boots and a sack with a string to tie it at the top and you shall see that it was a lucky day for you when you became my master."

The cat quickly went to catch some mice and rats to prove how useful he was, and the miller's son found him the boots and the sack which tied at the top. The cat was as pleased as punch with the boots and strutted around proudly. Then, taking the sack, he filled it with bran and tempting green leaves and set out for a nearby field where he knew there were many rabbits. There he lay down with the sack open beside him and pretended to be asleep.

Before long some curious rabbits came to investigate the sleeping cat and the sack, and when they smelt the delicious food they hopped into the sack. In a flash Puss-in-Boots jumped up, pulled the string tight, and caught the rabbits.

Now he strode off to the king's palace and demanded to see the king. "I have a gift for him from my master, the Marquis of Carabas," he announced. This was a name he had made up for the miller's son to impress the king. The king accepted the sack of rabbits graciously and sent a message to the cat's master thanking him for his kindness.

Some time later Puss-in-Boots set out again with his sack. This time he put a handful of corn in the sack and caught some partridge, and once more he took them to the king's palace, and presented them to the king from the Marquis of Carabas.

Not long afterwards Puss-in-Boots heard that the king was going to drive with his daughter by the river, and he told the miller's son to follow him and do whatever he said. By now the lad realized that Puss was no ordinary cat, and he promised to do everything he was told.

Puss then asked the miller's son to take off his clothes and swim in the river. When the king's carriage came past he called out, "Help, help! My master, the Marquis of Carabas, is drowning!" The king recognized the Marquis's name, stopped his carriage, and ordered his guards to save the young man. While they were dragging him out, the cat told the king, "He was attacked by thieves who have taken all his clothes." The truth was that Puss had hidden the clothes under a stone.

The king sent one of his servants to fetch some fine clothes, for the Marquis of Carabas had been very generous to him in the past. When the servants returned and the miller's son put on the new clothes he looked very handsome indeed. The king's daughter

immediately fell in love with him, and the king graciously asked if he would like to drive with them in their carriage.

While the king was talking to the miller's son and the king's daughter was falling in love with him, Puss ran on ahead, and found some men working in a field. "The king is about to drive past," he told them. "If he asks you who owns this field, you must answer 'The Marquis of Carabas'. If you don't," he added ferociously, "I shall make sure you are killed and chopped into little pieces."

A few moments later the king's carriage came along and the king asked the men who owned the land. They remembered the fierce threats from Puss-in-Boots and answered, "The Marquis of Carabas, Sire."

The king was impressed. Again the cat ran ahead and found some harvesters cutting corn. He told them to say all the fields they were working in belonged to the Marquis of Carabas. If they did not, he said he would make sure they were killed. When the king heard that the Marquis of Carabas owned this land too he was even more impressed.

Meanwhile Puss hurried on to a big castle where a wicked magician lived. The magician was the real owner of the land through which the king and his companions were driving.

The cat knocked at the door and asked to see the magician, and when he met him he bowed very low. "Is it true that you can change yourself into any animal – a lion, a tiger, even an elephant?" he asked with great respect.

"It is true," replied the magician and instantly turned into a great lion, and chased the cat. Puss-in-Boots was terrified and only just managed to scramble to safety on a roof – not easy for a cat wearing big boots. There he huddled until the lion changed back into the magician.

"That was truly remarkable," he said to the magician most politely. "But I don't suppose you can also turn yourself into a tiny animal like a mouse or a rat?"

"That's even easier," said the magician, and in a flash he became a tiny mouse, scampering on the floor. With a leap Puss pounced on him and that was the end of the magician.

Just then Puss-in-Boots heard the king's carriage arriving at the castle, so he went to the entrance and bowed low.

"Welcome to the house of my master, the Marquis of Carabas," he announced.

The king entered with his daughter and the miller's son and looked round at the fine castle. Knowing that his daughter already loved the young man, he said, "Tell me, Marquis, what would you say to marrying my daughter?"

The miller's son, who had fallen deeply in love with the princess, replied, "With all my heart I would like to."

The young man and his princess lived happily in the castle for many years, and you may be sure Puss-in-Boots was always well fed and well looked after for the rest of his life.

A Lion in the Meadow

Margaret Mahy

The little boy said, "Mother, there is a lion in the meadow."
The mother said, "Nonsense, little boy."

The little boy said, "Mother, there is a big yellow lion in the meadow."

The mother said, "Nonsense, little boy."

The little boy said, "Mother, there is a big, roaring, yellow, whiskery lion in the meadow!"

The mother said, "Little boy, you are making up stories again. There is nothing in the meadow but grass and trees. Go into the meadow and see for yourself."

The little boy said, "Mother, I'm scared to go into the meadow, because of the lion which is there."

The mother said, "Little boy, you are making up stories – so I will make up a story too . . . Do you see this match box? Take it out into the meadow and open it. In it will be a tiny dragon. The tiny dragon will grow into a big dragon. It will chase the lion away."

The little boy took the match box and went away. The mother went on peeling the potatoes.

Suddenly the door opened.

In rushed a big, roaring, yellow, whiskery lion.

"Hide me!" it said. "A dragon is after me!"

The lion hid in the broom closet.

Then the little boy came running in.

"Mother," he said. "That dragon grew too big. There is no lion in the meadow now. There is a DRAGON in the meadow."

The little boy hid in the broom closet too.

"You should have left me alone," said the lion. "I eat only apples."

"But there wasn't a real dragon," said the mother. "It was just a story I made up."

"It turned out to be true after all," said the little boy. "You should have looked in the match box first."

"That is how it is," said the lion. "Some stories are true, and some aren't. But I have an idea. We will go and play in the meadow on the other side of the house. There is no dragon there."

"I am glad we are friends now," said the little boy.

The little boy and the big roaring, yellow, whiskery lion went to play in the other meadow. The dragon stayed where he was, and nobody minded.

The mother never ever made up a story again.

The Black Bull of Norroway

Long ago, in a country far away in the north there lived a widow and her three daughters. She had once been a queen, but her husband, the king, had been killed in battle and she was now very, very poor.

One day her eldest daughter said to her, "Mother, bake me a cake to take to the fortune-teller so that she will tell me my fortune."

The fortune-teller accepted the fine cake the girl had brought, and then she said to her, "Stand by the back door, my dear, and tell me if anything comes down the road," By and by the girl cried out that a carriage drawn by six gray horses was coming towards them.

"Go with it," said the fortune-teller, "for there your fortune lies." The coachman stopped for the girl to climb in, and away they went.

Before long the second daughter asked her mother to bake a cake for the fortune-teller, for she too wanted to know what life had to offer her. "Stand by the back door, my dear," said the fortune-teller, "and tell me if anything comes down the road." Then, when a carriage drawn by six gleaming chestnut horses came by, she told the girl to get into it, for there lay her fortune.

In time the youngest daughter asked her mother to bake a cake for her to take to the fortune-teller. Just as before, the fortune-teller said, "Stand by the back door, my dear, and tell me if anything comes down the road." Soon the girl said,

"I can see a great black bull coming down the road."

"Go with the bull, girl," said the fortune-teller, "for your fortune lies with the bull."

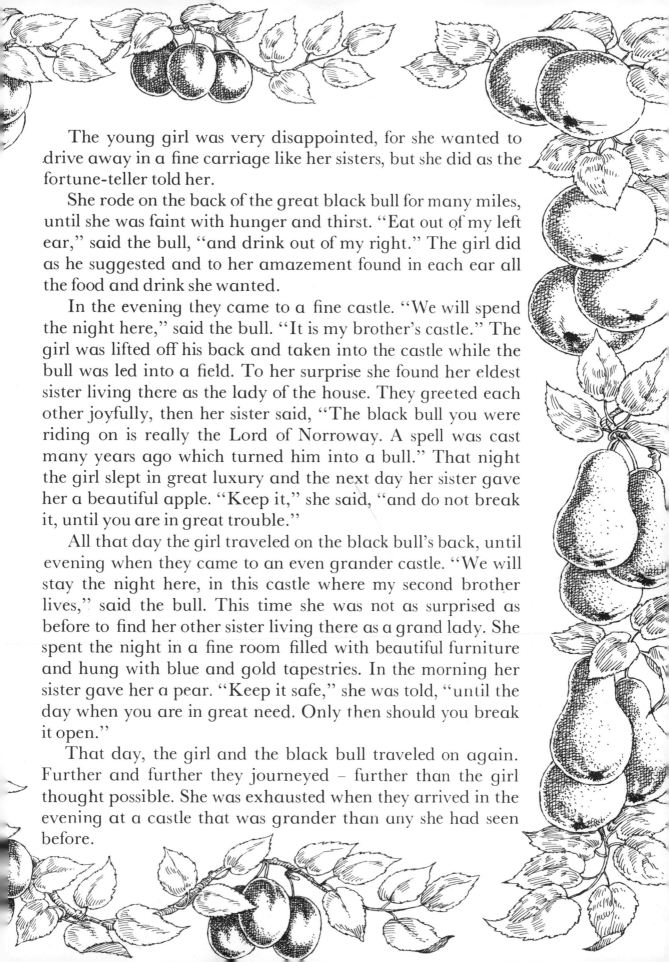

The young girl was very disappointed, for she wanted to drive away in a fine carriage like her sisters, but she did as the fortune-teller told her.

She rode on the back of the great black bull for many miles, until she was faint with hunger and thirst. "Eat out of my left ear," said the bull, "and drink out of my right." The girl did as he suggested and to her amazement found in each ear all the food and drink she wanted.

In the evening they came to a fine castle. "We will spend the night here," said the bull. "It is my brother's castle." The girl was lifted off his back and taken into the castle while the bull was led into a field. To her surprise she found her eldest sister living there as the lady of the house. They greeted each other joyfully, then her sister said, "The black bull you were riding on is really the Lord of Norroway. A spell was cast many years ago which turned him into a bull." That night the girl slept in great luxury and the next day her sister gave her a beautiful apple. "Keep it," she said, "and do not break it, until you are in great trouble."

All that day the girl traveled on the black bull's back, until evening when they came to an even grander castle. "We will stay the night here, in this castle where my second brother lives," said the bull. This time she was not as surprised as before to find her other sister living there as a grand lady. She spent the night in a fine room filled with beautiful furniture and hung with blue and gold tapestries. In the morning her sister gave her a pear. "Keep it safe," she was told, "until the day when you are in great need. Only then should you break it open."

That day, the girl and the black bull traveled on again. Further and further they journeyed – further than the girl thought possible. She was exhausted when they arrived in the evening at a castle that was grander than any she had seen before.

"This is my home," said the bull, "and we will stay here for tonight." The girl was well looked after as before and the next morning she was given a beautiful plum.

"Keep this carefully," she was told, "until the day when you are in great need. Only then should you break it open."

On the fourth day the great black bull took her to a deep dark valley, where he asked her to get off his back. "You must stay here," he said, "while I go and fight the devil. You will know if I win, for everything around will turn blue, but if I lose, everything you see will turn red. Sit on this boulder and remember you must not move, not even a hand or a foot until I return. For if you move, I shall never find you again."

The girl promised to do as she was told, for by now she loved and trusted the bull. For hours and hours she sat on the boulder without moving, then, just when she felt she could wait no longer, everything around her suddenly went blue. She was so delighted that she moved one foot. She moved it only a little, just enough to cross it over the other, forgetting her promise for a moment.

The bull returned after his victory but, just as he had said, he could not find her anywhere. The girl stayed in the valley for hours, weeping for what she had done, and at last she set off alone, although she did not know where to go.

After she had wandered from valley to valley for several days, the young girl came to a glass mountain. She tried to climb it, but each time her feet slipped backwards, and eventually she gave up. Soon after this she met a blacksmith who told her that if she worked for him for seven years he would make her special shoes of iron that would take her over the glass mountain.

For seven long years she worked hard for the blacksmith, and at the end of that time he kept his promise and made her the shoes to take her on her way. On the other side of the mountain she stopped at a little house where a washerwoman and her daughter were scrubbing some bloodstained clothes in a tub.

"The finest lord I have ever seen left these clothes here seven years ago," said the washerwoman. "He told us that whoever washed out the bloodstains would be his wife. But for seven long years we have washed and rinsed, and the stains remain."

"Let me try," said the girl, and the first time she washed the clothes the bloodstains disappeared. Absolutely delighted, the washerwoman rushed off and told the lord of the castle nearby that the clothes were clean. Now this lord was the Lord of Norroway, and the old woman lied to him, saying that it was her own daughter who had done the task. She thought it would be a fine thing for her daughter to marry a lord. The wedding was arranged for the next day, and there seemed nothing the young girl could do to stop it.

Then she remembered the apple she had been given so long ago. Surely the time had come to open it. Inside were jewels, which sparkled and shone. She showed these to the washerwoman, and asked if she could see the lord alone that evening. "The jewels will all be yours if you arrange this for me," she said. The washerwoman took the jewels greedily, but before she allowed the girl to go to the lord's room, she put a sleeping potion in his drink, so that he slept deeply the whole night through. The girl sat by his bedside, and she cried,

> "Seven long years I served for thee,
> The glassy hill I climbed for thee,
> The blood-stained clothes I washed for thee,
> Wilt thou not wake, and turn to me?"

but the Lord of Norroway slept on.

The next day the girl was overcome with grief, for she could not think how to stop the wedding, so she broke open the pear, and found it contained even more lovely jewels than the apple. She took these once again to the washerwoman. "Marry your daughter' tomorrow," she begged, "not today, and let me see the lord alone once more. In return the jewels will be yours." The washerwoman agreed, but again slipped a sleeping potion into the lord's drink.

For the second time the girl tried to waken the Lord of Norroway.

> "Seven long years I served for thee,
> The glassy hill I climbed for thee,
> The blood-stained clothes I washed for thee,
> Wilt thou not wake and turn to me?"

she cried over and over again, but he slept on, the whole night through.

The next morning the girl broke open the beautiful plum she had been given, and found an even greater collection of splendid jewels. She offered them to the greedy washerwoman who agreed to put off the wedding for one more day. That night, while allowing the girl to visit the bridegroom, she once more put the sleeping potion into his drink. But this time the lord poured away the drink when the washerwoman was not looking for he suspected trickery of some kind. When the girl came to his room for the third time and cried,

"Seven long years I served for thee,
The glassy hill I climbed for thee,
The blood-stained clothes I washed for thee,
Wilt thou not wake and turn to me?"

he turned and saw her.

As they talked he told her his story: how a spell had been cast on him turning him into a bull, how he had fought and beaten the devil and the spell had been broken. "Ever since then," he said, "I have been searching for you."

The Lord of Norroway and the youngest daughter were married next day, and lived happily in the castle. "I little thought," she said, "the day I saw the black bull coming down the road, that I had truly found my fortune."

How the Whale Became

Ted Hughes

Now God had a little garden. In this garden he grew carrots, onions, beans and whatever else he needed for his dinner. It was a fine little garden. The plants were in neat rows, and a tidy fence kept out the animals. God was pleased with it.

One day as he was weeding the carrots he saw a strange thing between the rows. It was no more than an inch long, and it was black. It was like a black shiny bean. At one end it had a little root going into the ground.

"That's very odd," said God. "I've never seen one of these before. I wonder what it will grow into."

So he left it growing.

Next day, as he was gardening, he remembered the little shiny black thing. He went to see how it was getting on. He was surprised. During the night it had doubled its length. It was now two inches long, like a shiny black egg.

Every day God went to look at it, and every day it was bigger. Every morning, in fact, it was just twice as long as it had been the morning before.

When it was six feet long, God said :

"It's getting too big. I must pull it up and cook it."

But he left it a day.

Next day it was twelve feet long and far too big to go into any of God's pans.

God stood scratching his head and looking at it. Already it had crushed most of his carrots out of sight. It it went on growing at this rate it would soon be pushing his house over.

Suddenly, as he looked at it, it opened an eye and looked at him.

God was amazed.

The eye was quite small and round. It was near the thickest end, and farthest from the root. He walked round to the other side, and there was another eye, also looking at him.

"Well!" said God. "And how do you do?"

The round eye blinked, and the smooth glossy skin under it wrinkled slightly, as if the thing was smiling. But there was no mouth, so God wasn't sure.

Next morning God rose early and went out into his garden.

Sure enough, during the night his new black plant with eyes had doubled its length again. It had pushed down part of his fence, so that its head was sticking out into the road, one eye looking up it, and one down. Its side was pressed against the kitchen wall.

God walked round to its front and looked it in the eye.

"You are too big," he said sternly. "Please stop growing before you push my house down."

To his surprise, the plant opened a mouth. A long slit of a mouth, which ran back on either side under the eyes.

"I can't," said the mouth.

God didn't know what to say. At last he said:

"Well then, can you tell me what sort of a thing you are? Do you know?"

"I," said the thing, "am Whale-Wort. You have heard of Egg-plant, and Buck-Wheat, and Dog-Daisy. Well, I am Whale-Wort."

There was nothing God could do about that.

By next morning, Whale-Wort stretched right across the road, and his side had pushed the kitchen wall into the kitchen. He was now longer and fatter than a bus.

When God saw this, he called the creatures together.

"Here's a strange thing," he said. "Look at it. What are we going to do with it?"

The creatures walked round Whale-Wort, looking at him. His skin was so shiny they could see their faces in it.

"Leave it," suggested Ostrich. "And wait till it dies down."

"But it might go on growing," said God. "Until it covers the whole earth. We shall have to live on its back. Think of that."

"I suggest," said Mouse, "that we throw it into the sea."

God thought.

"No," he said at last. "That's too severe. Let's just leave it for a few days."

After three more days, God's house was completely flat, and Whale-Wort was as long as a street.

"Now," said Mouse, "it is too late to throw it into the sea. Whale-Wort is too big to move."

But God fastened long thick ropes round him and called up all the creatures to help haul on the ends.

"Hey!" cried Whale-Wort. "Leave me alone."

"You are going into the sea," cried Mouse. "And it serves you right. Taking up all this space."

"But I'm happy!" cried Whale-Wort again. "I'm happy just lying here. Leave me and let me sleep. I was made just to lie and sleep."

"Into the sea!" cried Mouse.

"No!" cried Whale-Wort.

"Into the sea!" cried all the creatures. And they hauled on the ropes. With a great groan, Whale-Wort's root came out of the ground. He began to thresh and twist, beating down houses and trees with his long root, as the creatures dragged him willy-nilly through the countryside.

At last they got him to the top of a high cliff. With a great shout they rolled him over the edge and into the sea.

"Help! Help!" cried Whale-Wort. "I shall drown! Please let me come back on land where I can sleep."

"Not until you're smaller!" shouted God. "Then you can come back."

"But how am I to get smaller?" wept Whale-Wort, as he rolled to and fro in the sea. "Please show me how to get smaller so that I can live on land."

God bent down from the high cliff and poked Whale-Wort on the top of his head with his finger.

"Ow!" cried Whale-Wort. "What was that for? You've made a hole. The water will come in."

"No it won't" said God. "But some of you will come out. Now just you start blowing some of yourself out through that hole."

Whale-Wort blew, and a high jet of spray shot up out of the hole that God had made.

"Now go on blowing," said God.

Whale-Wort blew and blew. Soon he was quite a bit smaller. As he shrank, his skin, that had been so tight and glossy, became covered with tiny wrinkles. At last God said to him:

"When you're as small as a cucumber, just give a shout. Then you can come back into my garden. But until then, you shall stay in the sea."

And God walked away with all his creatures, leaving Whale-Wort rolling and blowing in the sea.

Soon Whale-Wort was down to the size of a bus. But blowing was hard work, and by this time he felt like a sleep. He took a deep breath and sank down to the bottom of the sea for a sleep. Above all, he loved to sleep.

When he awoke he gave a roar of dismay. While he was asleep he had grown back to the length of a street and the fatness of a ship with two funnels.

He rose to the surface as fast as he could and began to blow. Soon he was back down to the size of a truck. But soon, too, he felt like another sleep. He took a deep breath and sank to the bottom.

When he awoke he was back to the length of a street.

This went on for years. It is still going on.

As fast as Whale-Wort shrinks with blowing, he grows with sleeping. Sometimes, when he is feeling very strong, he gets himself down to the size of an automobile. But always before he gets himself down to the size of a cucumber, he remembers how nice it is to sleep. When he wakes, he has grown again.

He longs to come back on land and sleep in the sun, with his root in the earth. But instead of that, he must roll and blow, out on the wild sea. And until he is allowed to come back on land, the creatures call him just Whale.

The Traveling Musicians

One day an old donkey overheard his master saying that he was too old for work. The time had come for him to be killed off for they could not keep an animal who was no longer useful.

"Killed indeed!" snorted the donkey. "I may be too old to carry heavy loads but I am not too old to make a fine noise when I bray. I shall go to the neighboring town of Bremen and earn my keep there as a musician."

He unlatched the stable door with his teeth, a trick he had learned long ago, and when no one was looking he slipped out and trotted down the road towards Bremen.

He had not gone far when he saw an old dog lying by the side of the road looking rather sorry for himself.

"Why so sad, Dog?" he asked.

"You would feel just as sad if you had overheard your master say he was going to knock you on the head because you were too old."

"Come with me, friend," said the donkey. "I am also too old for my master, so I am off to Bremen to earn my living as a musician. You can use your voice, can't you? Together we will sing a fine duet."

The dog agreed to travel to Bremen with the donkey, and they trotted down the road together. Before long, they saw a cat hunched up and miserable sitting on a gate.

"It's a fine day, Cat," they said, "too fine for you to look so sad."

"It's a bad sad day for me," said the cat. "My owners say I no longer catch as many rats and mice as I did when I was young, so they are replacing me with a kitten. What is more, they said they could not afford to feed us both, so I am going to be put in a sack with a stone and drowned in the river."

"Don't wait for that to happen," said the donkey and the dog. "We are also too old for our masters, but we have not waited to be finished off. We are on our way to Bremen to earn our living as musicians. You still have your voice. Come with us."

The cat uttered a fine "Meow!" in agreement.

So the three animals journeyed on to Bremen together. At the next farm they met a cock strutting up and down. All his feathers were ruffled out in indignation.

"What's the trouble, Cock?" they asked. "You look upset."

"How would you feel," replied the cock, "if you overheard your mistress planning to wring your neck so she could eat you for dinner on Sunday when they have visitors coming?"

"Come with us to Bremen," said the donkey, the dog and the cat. "We are going to earn our living there as musicians. We're sure you have a fine singing voice."

"Indeed I do," said the cock, and to show them he uttered a loud "Cock-a-doodle-doo!"

It was too far for them to reach Bremen that day, so when evening came they found a sheltered place in a wood to rest for the night. The dog and the donkey settled themselves comfortably at the bottom of a tree, the cat climbed into the branches, and the cock roosted high up at the top. They were all tired, but none of them slept for they were all so hungry.

When it was quite dark the animals saw a light shining from a nearby house they had not noticed before. It made them think of

food, and towards midnight the cat said, "Friends, let's go and investigate. Where there is a house, there may be something to eat."

Together they crept up to one of the windows where a light was shining. The donkey being the tallest looked through first.

"Well, friend, what do you see?" asked the cock.

"I see a table laden with food and drink, and a group of mean-looking men counting piles of money," said the donkey.

The cat, the dog and cockerel now jumped up onto the donkey's back and peered through the window too. They did not realize it but they had discovered a robber's hideout hidden deep in the woods.

"Let us try out our music," said one of the animals. "If we sing a fine song for them they may give us some of their supper."

Together they all sang. The donkey brayed, the dog barked, the cat yowled and the cock crowed. The noise was tremendous.

The effect was not at all what they expected, for the robbers, hearing this noise, thought they were about to be arrested. They ran helter-skelter as fast as they could into the woods, leaving the doors wide open.

"That was nice of them," said the four animals, when the robbers did not reappear. "They have gone away and left us their home to enjoy."

The donkey found some good hay in the barn and the cock some grain, while the cat and the dog ate all they wanted from the robbers' table. Then all slept soundly. In time the candles burned down and went out and the house lay in darkness.

Some hours later, the robbers returned. They had been arguing among themselves, for some thought they had given in too easily, by running away without a fight, while the others thought it was foolish to go back to the house, for they would surely be caught and put in prison. Now they drew nearer, and seeing no sign of life decided it would be safe for one of them to return and at least take some of the gold they had left behind.

Quietly the robber crept up to the house, and tried to light a candle. As he did so the cat awoke, and the robber saw his green eyes glowing in the dark. Mistaking them for the embers of the fire, he held out a splinter of wood to them.

The cat, thinking he was being attacked, flew at the robber, spitting and scratching for all he was worth. The robber, fearing some great wild beast was attacking him, dropped the wood and ran for his life. In the doorway he tripped over the dog who immediately bit the robber's ankle and howled in agony from the kick he had received. The robber ran headlong across the yard where the donkey lashed out his heels as he went past. The cock, hearing all the commotion and fearing his friends were being killed flew at the stranger, flapping his wings around his head, stretching out his claws and screeching all the time.

The robber fled back to his companions. "It is surely a monster and a devil rolled into one that has taken over our house," he said. "First I was scratched, then bitten, then kicked, and finally attacked from above by fierce talons and whirling feathers. The noise of screeching and howling was enough to wake the dead. We must never go back there again."

So it was that the robbers set off to another part of the country and left their hideout in the woods to the animals. Meanwhile the four musicians discussed in the morning the strange disturbances in the middle of the night. Since the intruder had disappeared they decided to stay where they were for a time.

"We will go to Bremen another day," they said.

But they never did go to Bremen. Instead they lived happily in the house for many years and never tried singing together again.

The Little House

Once upon a time a large earthenware jar rolled off the back of a cart that was going to market. It came to rest in the grass at the side of the road.

By and by a mouse came along and looked at the jar. "What a fine house that would make," he thought, and he called out:

"Little house, little house,
Who lives in the little house?"

Nobody answered so the mouse peeped in and saw that it was empty. He moved in straight away and began to live there.

Before long a frog came along and saw the jar. "What a fine house that would make," he thought and he called out:

"Little house, little house,
Who lives in the little house?"
and he heard:

"I, Mr Mouse.
I live in the little house.
Who are you?"

"I am Mr Frog," came the reply.

"Come in Mr Frog, and we can live here together," called out the mouse.

So the mouse and the frog lived happily together in the little house. Then one day a hare came running along the road and saw the little house. He called out:

"Little house, little house,
Who lives in the little house?"

And he heard:
    "Mr Frog and Mr Mouse,
    We live in the little house.
    Who are you?"
    "I am Mr Hare," he replied.
    "Come in Mr Hare and live with us," called the mouse and the frog.
    The hare went in and settled down with the frog and the mouse in the little house.
    Some time later a fox came along, and spied the little house. "That would make a fine house," he thought and he called out:
    "Little house, little house,
    Who lives in the little house?"
and he heard:
    "Mr Hare, Mr Frog and Mr Mouse,
    We all live in the little house.
    Who are you?"
    "I am Mr Fox," he replied.
    "Then come in and live with us, Mr Fox," they called back.
    Mr Fox went in and found there was just room for him too, although it was a bit of a squeeze.
    The next day a bear came ambling along the road, and saw the little house. He called out:
    "Little house, little house,
    Who lives in the little house?"
and he heard:
    "Mr Fox, Mr Hare, Mr Frog and Mr Mouse,
    We all live in the little house.
    Who are you?"
    "I am Mr Bear Squash-you-all-flat," said the bear.
    He then sat down on the little house, and squashed it all flat.
    That was the end of the little house.

Pegasus the Winged Horse

Long, long ago, there lived the fiercest monster imaginable, called the Chimera. He had three heads, each of them different, and could breathe fire from all three mouths at once. One head was shaped like a goat, one like a lion, and the third was in the form of a serpent. All might have been well if the monster had lived quietly in the mountains, but he was so fierce and so hungry, he was forever coming down into the cities and villages, eating people, destroying buildings and burning up crops on the farms. No one could get near enough to kill him, for his flames reached out too far. It looked as though the whole of mankind would be destroyed by the Chimera.

The king of the country where the Chimera did so much damage offered a great reward to anyone who would rid him of this monster. There was a young man called Bellerophon, who wanted to prove his bravery, and so he came forward. He had an idea that if he could attack the monster from the air he might have a chance of winning.

One night, in a dream, Athene, the Goddess of Wisdom, came to Bellerophon and told him about Pegasus, the winged horse of the gods, of the fountain where the horse liked to drink, and where he might find a golden bridle which would help him tame the horse. So Bellerophon went to the fountain and found the bridle of gold, and hid until Pegasus came to drink. He was such a lovely horse that Bellerophon almost forgot to catch him, but as Pegasus was drinking, he crept up and slipped the reins over the horse's neck.

Pegasus, who had never been touched by a man before, jumped away, and as he did so Bellerophon leaped on to his back. A great struggle took place between them for Pegasus tried every trick he knew to throw Bellerophon. He soared up into the sky; he twisted, bucked, reared, spun around. Somehow Bellerophon hung on, and at last he was able to get the bit into Pegasus' mouth. Soon after this Pegasus gave in and came to rest on the ground, his sides heaving with exhaustion.

Bellerophon explained to the beautiful white winged horse why he had captured him, and how he needed his help to save the kingdom from the fire-eating monster. As he spoke, he saw that there were tears in the horse's eyes, and said, "I cannot do this to you. It is no quarrel of yours. You shall go free and I must find some other way to win this victory." He took off the bridle and watched Pegasus soar into the sky.

In a few minutes, just as he was about to start his journey home, he felt a gentle nuzzle by his arm. To Bellerophon's amazement and delight, the horse had returned of his own free will.

For many days they trained together so that they would have the best possible chance against the Chimera. At last, the day came. Bellerophon took out his finest armor, sharpened his sword and set out with Pegasus to slay the monster.

The Chimera was outside his cave, preparing to raid another village, for he was feeling hungry. Before he knew what was happening, and without hearing more than a faint whirr in the air above him, he felt an agonizing blow. Bellerophon had chopped off one of his heads. It was the goat's head, and it lay in the dust while the monster roared with pain and lashed his tail with rage. Smoke and flames shot out in every direction as he tried to find his attacker.

Hidden by the smoke, Pegasus and Bellerophon were able to swoop down on him again and in a flash the sword swept through another neck. This time the lion's head rolled in the dust. The monster was wild and savage with pain and anger. He hurled himself at his attackers, and clung to Pegasus with his huge scaly claws as the horse rose into the air. Bellerophon thought they would surely die; the heat from the flames was terrible, and the serpent's head was only inches from his own. But the horse never wavered, soaring higher and higher into the air.

As the serpent's head stretched out to strike, Bellerophon saw a weak spot under its neck and drove his sword in with all his strength. The Chimera gave a ghastly scream. His hold on Pegasus loosened and he tumbled backwards in a shower of sparks. He crashed to the ground burning as he went.

Bellerophon became a great hero, and so did the winged horse. They had other adventures together, but when Bellerophon tried to fly to heaven with Pegasus he was thrown. Some people said that Zeus, the king of the gods, was jealous, and sent an insect to tickle Pegasus and make him throw his rider. Pegasus went on flying up to heaven where he was changed into a group of stars, which you may see if you are lucky.

Sam Pig and the Wind

Alison Uttley

It was washing day and Ann Pig decided that it was time Sam Pig's pants were put in the washtub. They were new pants, made of sheep's wool, dyed red and blue in large checks, but they were dirty, for Sam had fallen into a pool of mud and stuck there till he was rescued.

So Ann scrubbed and rubbed them and hung them up to dry on the clothes-line in the crab-apple orchard, where they fluttered among pajamas and handkerchiefs and the rest of the family wash.

Sam Pig stood near watching them, for he was afraid the Fox might steal them if he got the chance. It was a warm day, and Sam enjoyed having his little legs free.

"I'll stand on guard," said he, "then nobody can take my pants for their nests or anything."

The pair of pants bobbed and danced on the clothes-line as if somebody were shaking them. It was the wind, which was blowing strongly. It came out of the clouds with a sudden swoop, and it puffed them and it huffed them, and it stuffed them with air. They really seemed to have a pair of invisible fat legs inside them as they swung to and fro and jigged and turned somersaults over the line.

The wind must have taken a fancy to those pants for it gave a great tug and the wooden clothespins fell to the ground. Sam Pig stooped to pick up his pants, but they leaped away out of his grasp, and across the orchard. Sam sprang after them in a hurry.

They frisked over the wall, struggled among the rough stones, and disappeared. Sam was sure they would be lying on the other side, and he climbed slowly and carefully to the top. Alas! The little pants were already running swiftly across the meadow, trundling along the ground as if a pair of stout legs were inside them. Sam jumped down and ran after them at full speed. He nearly reached them, for the wind dropped and the little pants flapped and fell empty to the ground. Just as Sam's arm was outstretched to grab them the wind swept down with a howl and caught them up again. It whirled them higher and higher, and tossed them into a tree.

"Whoo-oo-oo," whistled the wind, as it shook them and left them. There they dangled, caught in a branch. Sam Pig was not daunted. He began to climb that tree. He was part way up, clasping the slippery trunk, when the pants disentangled themselves and fell to the earth.

"Hurrah!" cried Sam, and he slithered down to safety. "Hurrah! Now I can get them."

No! The wind swept down upon them. They rose on their little balloon legs and danced away. The wind blew stronger, and the trousers took leaps in the air like an acrobat. They turned head over heels; they danced on one leg and then on the other, like a sailor doing the hornpipe.

"Give me back my pants, O wind," called Sam Pig, and the wind laughed. "Who-o-o-o. Who-o-o-o," and shrieked, "Noo-oo-oo," in such a shrill high voice that Sam shivered with the icy coldness of it.

The pants jigged along the meadows and into the woods, with Sam running breathlessly after them. He tripped over brambles and caught his feet in rabbit holes, but the pants leaped over the briars, and escaped the thorns as the wind tugged them away. When the wind paused a moment to take a deep breath Sam Pig got near, but he was never in time to catch the runaways.

"What's the matter, Sam?" asked the gray donkey when Sam ran past with his arms outstretched and his ears laid flat. "Why are you running so fast?"

"My pants! My pants!" panted Sam. "The wind's got them, and it's blowing them away."

"My goodness! It will blow them across the world, Sam. You'll never see them again," cried the donkey. He kicked up his heels and brayed loudly and then galloped after them with his teeth bared.

"Hee-haw! Hee-haw! Stop! Stop!" he blared in his trumpet voice. But he couldn't catch them either, so he returned to his thistles.

The pants were now running across a cornfield, and as they leaped over the stubble Sam was sure there was somebody inside them. It was an airy fellow, whose long transparent arms and sea-green fingers waved and pointed to sky and earth. A laughing mocking face with puffed-out cheeks nodded at Sam, and a pursed-up mouth whistled shrilly.

"Catch me! Catch me! Get me if you can! I'm the wind, Sam Pig. The wind! I'm the wind from the World's End."

"Wait a minute," said Sam, rather crossly, and he trundled along on his fat little legs.

The wind turned round and danced about Sam, pulling his tail and blowing in his face so that the little pig had to shut his eyes. Suddenly the wind blew a hurricane. It picked him up and carried him in the air. How frightened was our little Sam Pig when he felt his feet paddling on nothing! His curly tail stuck out straight, his ears were flattened, his body cold as ice. He tried to call for help but no words came.

Then the wind took pity on him, and dropped him lightly to the ground. He gave a pitiful squeak and lay panting and puffing with fright. He opened his eyes and saw his pants lying near. He edged towards them and put out a hand, but the pants stood up, shook themselves full of air, and went dancing off.

Sam Pig arose and followed after. He was a strong-hearted little pig and he was determined not to lose his beloved pants.

The wind carried them to the farmyard, and sent them fluttering their flapping sides among the hens. The cock crowed, the hens all ran helter-skelter, and the pants trotted here and there among them, ruffling their feathers, blowing them about like leaves.

"Stop it! Catch it! Catch the wind!" cried Sam.

"Nobody can catch the wind," crowed the cock. "Cockadoodle doo! Take shelter, my little red wives!" And the little hens crouched together in a bunch.

"Puff! Puff! Whoo-oo-oo!" screamed the wind, blowing out its cheeks, and prancing in the little check pants belonging to Sam Pig.

The wind blew in a sudden gust and the pants flew over the gate into the field where Sally the mare grazed. With a whoop and a cry the wind seized her mane and dragged at her long tail. She turned her back and even when the little pants leaped to her haunches, she took no notice.

"Get on! Gee-up! Whoo-oo-oo to you," cried the wind, angrily kicking her ribs with invisible toes, and thumping her sides with the empty legs of the check pants. The mare stood stock still, head bent, refusing to budge an inch. Sam Pig came hurrying up to his old friend.

"O Sally! Catch the wind! Keep the wind from taking my pants away. Hold it, Sally!"

"You can't catch the wind, little Sam. It's free to blow where it likes, and nobody can tame it," muttered Sally. "But I won't move for any wind that blows."

So the wind leapt away and skipped across the fields. The long grasses all turned with it, and tried to follow, but the earth held them back.

The wind blew next along a country lane, and the little pants scampered between the flowery banks with Sam Pig following after. They reached the high road, and Sam hesitated for a moment, but he was determined to catch his check pants.

Clouds of white dust rose and came after them, and pieces of paper were caught and whirled in the air.

An old woman walked along the road. Her shawl was tightly wrapped around her shoulders, her bonnet fastened with a ribbon, and her black shoes latched on her feet. In her hand she grasped a green umbrella of prodigious size. It was the old witch woman going to the village to do her marketing.

"Drat the wind! It's raising a mighty dust! It will spoil my best bonnet," she murmured to herself as she saw the cloud of white dust sweeping upon her. She opened the big umbrella and held it over her bonnet. But the wind shot out a long arm and grasped the green umbrella. It snatched it from her hand and bore it away inside out.

She gave a cry of dismay and bent her head to keep her bonnet from being torn from its ribbons.

"My poor old umbereller! It's gone! It's seen many a storm of wind and rain, but never a gust as sharp as this!"

The wind passed on, and she ventured to raise her eyes. In the distance she could see the green umbrella flying along, and a pair of pants running under it, and after them a short fat pig.

The wind and Sam came to a church with a weathercock on top of the tower. The iron cock looked down in alarm. It spun round on its creaking axis, and crackled its stiff feathers. Backwards went the wind, and back went the weathercock, and back went Sam Pig, and back went the pants and the umbrella and all. Away they went over the fields, taking the shortest cut, over the brook and up the hill. Sam Pig saw that the wind was heading for home.

There was the little house at the edge of the wood, and there the little stream with Ann filling the kettle, and there the drying-ground with the clothes-line, empty and forlorn between the crab-apple trees.

The wind bustled over the grass and stopped dead. The pair of pants fell in a heap. The green umbrella lay with its ribs sticking out. Its horn handle and thick cotton cover were unharmed for it had lived a hundred years already and weathered many a gale.

"Give me back my pants," said Sam, in a tired little voice.

"Take thy pants," answered the wind, and it shook the pants and dropped them again.

Sam Pig leaped with a last great effort upon his pants, and held them down. They never offered to move, for the wind had died away, and the air was still.

"Where are you, wind? Where have you gone?" asked Sam when he recovered himself sufficiently to speak. There was silence except for a faint whisper near the ground. Sam put his ear to a hare-bell's lip, and from it came the clear tiny tinkle of a baby wind which was curled up inside and going to sleep.

"Good-bye, Sam Pig," said this very small whisper of a voice. "Good-bye. I gave you a fine run, Sam Pig, and you were a good follower."

"Good-bye, wind," murmured Sam, and he sighed and lay down with his head on his pants. He fell asleep in a twinkling.

There Ann found him when she came to the orchard to collect the clothespins. On the ground lay Sam, with his face coated with dust, but smiling happily. His little feet were stained and cut, his arm outstretched over his torn pants. By him was a green umbrella, inside out.

Ann carefully turned it the right way. Then she stooped and gave her brother a shake.

"Sam! Sam! Wake up!" she called. "Sam! Where have you been?"

Sam rubbed his eyes and yawned. Then he sat up.

"Oh Sam! There was such a wind as you never saw! It blew the clothes off the line and I found them lying here, all except your pants. Oh, poor Sam! I thought it had blown them right away, but here they are, under your head."

"Yes, Ann," said Sam, yawning again. "The wind carried them off. I saw it with my own eyes. It ran a long, long way, but I ran too, and I caught it and got my pants again."

"You caught the wind? You got your pants back from the raging, roaring wind?" asked Ann in astonishment.

"Yes," Sam nodded proudly, and he opened his mouth, and shut it again. "I ran about a hundred miles. I raced the wind, and I wouldn't let it keep my pants."

"And what's this?" asked Ann, holding up the green umbrella.

"Oh, that belongs to the nice old witch woman. I passed her on the way, and the wind snatched it from her. I'll take it back some time. I'm so sleepy, Ann. Do leave me alone."

Sam's head dropped on the pants, and he fell fast asleep. So Badger carried him in and put him to bed. Ann mended the adventurous pants which the wind had torn. She turned out the pockets and found a small ancient whistle, which somebody had left there.

"Don't touch it," warned Badger. "Don't blow it. It's the wind's own whistle. Don't you know the saying 'Whistle for the wind'? If ever Sam wants the wind to come he has only to blow the whistle. We don't want it now, but if we ever do it will come."

The Little Jackal and the Crocodile

There was once a little jackal who lived in the jungle. He was a greedy little jackal, and one of his favorite meals was fresh crabs from the river. One day he went down to the big river near his home and put his paw in the water to pull out a crab.

Snap! A large, lazy crocodile who had been lying in the water snapped his jaws and caught the jackal's paw. The little jackal did not cry out, although he was very frightened. Instead he laughed.

"Ha! Ha! That crocodile in the river thinks he has caught my paw, but the stupid animal does not realize he has snapped up a piece of wood and is holding it in his jaws."

The crocodile immediately opened his mouth for he did not want to be seen with a log of wood in his jaws. Quickly the little jackal danced away and called cheekily from a safe distance, "I'll catch some crabs another day, Mr Crocodile." The crocodile lashed his tail with rage and resolved to catch the little jackal and eat him the next time he came to the river.

A week later, when his paw was healed, the jackal came back to the river. He wanted to catch some crabs, but did not want to be eaten by the crocodile. This time he called out from a safe distance, "I can't see any crabs lying on the bank, so I'll have to dip my paw into the water near the edge," and he watched the river for a few minutes. The crocodile thought, "Now is my chance to catch the jackal," and he swam close to the river bank.

When the little jackal saw the water move, he called out, "Thank you, Mr Crocodile. Now I know you are there, I'll come back another day."

The crocodile lashed his tail with rage until he stirred up the mud from the bottom of the river. He swore he would not let the little jackal trick him again.

The jackal could not stop thinking about the crabs, so a few days later he went down to the river again. He could not see the crocodile so he called out:

"I know crabs make bubbles in the water, so as soon as I see some bubbles I'll dip my paw in and then I'll catch them easily."

When he heard this, the crocodile, who was lying just beneath the water started to blow bubbles as fast as he could. He was sure that the jackal would put his paw in where the bubbles were rising and *Snap!* This time he would have the little jackal.

But when the jackal saw the bubbles, he called out:

"Thank you, Mr Crocodile, for showing me where you are. I'll come another day for the crabs."

The crocodile was so angry at being tricked again that he waited till the jackal's back was turned, then he jumped out of the river and followed the jackal, determined to catch him and eat him this time.

Now the jackal, who was very hungry, made his way to the fig grove to eat some figs. By the time the crocodile arrived, he was having a lovely feast munching the ripe blue fruit, and licking his lips with pleasure.

The crocodile was exhausted by walking on land which he found was much more difficult than swimming in the river. "I am too tired to catch the jackal now," he said to himself. "But I'll set a trap and catch him next time he comes for the figs."

The next day, the greedy jackal returned to the fig grove. He did love eating figs! To his surprise he saw a large and rather untidy pile of figs that had not been there before. "I wonder if my friend the crocodile has anything to do with this?" he said to himself, and he called out:

"What a lovely pile of figs! All I need to do is to see which figs wave in the breeze, for it is always the ripest and most delicious figs that wave in the breeze. I shall then know which ones to eat."

Of course the crocodile was buried under the pile of figs and and when he heard this he smiled a big toothy crocodile smile. "All I have to do is to wriggle a bit," he thought. "When the jackal sees the figs move he will come and eat them and this time I will certainly catch him."

The little jackal watched as the crocodile wriggled under the pile of figs, and he laughed and laughed.

"Thank you, Mr Crocodile," he said, "I'll come back another day when you are not here."

Now the crocodile was really in a rage so he followed the little jackal to his house to catch him there. There was no one at home when the crocodile got there, but the crocodile thought, "I will wait here, and catch him when he comes home tonight."

He was too big to go through the gate, so he broke it and then he was too big to go through the door, so he smashed that. "Never mind," he said to himself. "I will eat the little jackal tonight whatever happens," and he lay in wait for the jackal in the jackal's little house.

When the jackal came home he saw the broken gate, and smashed door, and he said to himself, "I wonder if my friend the crocodile has anything to do with this?" Then he called out:

"Little house, why haven't you said 'hello' to me as you do each night when I come home?"

The crocodile heard this, and thought he ought to make everything seem as normal as possible, so he shouted out, "Hello little jackal!"

Then a wicked smile appeared on the jackal's face. He fetched some twigs and branches, piled them up outside his house, and set fire to it. As the house burned he called out:

"A roast crocodile is safer than a live crocodile! I shall go and build myself a new house by the river where I can catch all the crabs I want."

With that he skipped off to the river bank and for all I know he is still there today, eating crabs all day long, and laughing at the way he tricked the crocodile.

The Great Flood

Long, long ago in a far off land there was a great flood. For days and weeks and months it rained and rained and rained. Puddles turned into lakes and tiny streams into great rivers and in time the whole earth was covered with water. This is the story of how it happened

At that time wicked people lived on the earth. They lived violent, evil lives. God saw this and was deeply hurt.

"I am sorry that I ever made the human race," God said. "I will end the whole dreadful business. I will destroy the people, the animals, the reptiles, the wild birds – everything."

But there was one family who made God pause for a moment. "Noah and his family," thought God. "No! I cannot destroy them. They are good people and love me. I know what I shall do."

Now Noah was a very old man and he and his wife had three sons called Shem, Ham and Japheth, all of whom were married. One day Noah was working in the fields when God appeared to him.

"Build a ship on dry land," God commanded him. "Build it high and broad and long. Make windows in it and a strong door in the side and build it with three decks, each divided into many compartments. Seal it, too, inside and out with pitch to keep it watertight."

"When the time comes, take into this great ark pairs of every animal – reptiles and birds as well – and enough food to feed them all. For I am going to send a flood of water over the whole land. I will destroy everything that lives except you and your family and the creatures with you in the ark."

Noah and his sons began to build the ark as God commanded them. For months they sawed down trees, cut them into planks and hammered them into place. The people who lived around them stared in amazement as the huge ship began to take shape, and laughed at them for working so hard. "Where are you going to sail that?" they jeered. "It's wider than the river."

But Noah and his sons worked on and at last the ship was ready. It had windows all around and a huge door on one side. Inside were three decks, each divided into different rooms. Some of these were filled with food of all kinds - flour and dried fruit, vegetables, grain and stacks of hay. Whatever Noah and his family could find, they stored in the ark.

Now the time came when God told Noah to call the animals and to tell his family to enter the great ship. And now two by two the animals came. There were great cats and tiny mice and the smallest of insects. There were antelope and horses, camels and rhinoceroses, lizards, snakes and tortoises. It took seven days for them all to arrive and soon the ark was very full indeed - the giraffes squashed up against the hippopotamuses and the

ostriches with the zebras, while the rafters above them were filled with roosting birds of all colors. On the seventh day as the elephants walked firmly up the gangway, rain splashed down on their gray hides and God told Noah to enter and close the ark.

Now the clouds grew darker and the rain began to fall more and more heavily. Never before had such rain been seen. It poured like a waterfall from the sky and the seas began to rise. Huge tidal waves flowed over the land, drowning everything in their path. Day after day it rained until all that could be seen was the ark floating on a vast gray sea above the land, above even the mountain tops.

At last the rain fell more gently and slowly the flood began to go down. The animals and Noah's family lived together for five months without sight of anything but water. Now they felt their ship settle on solid ground. They had come to rest on the top of a mountain called Ararat.

Noah peered anxiously out of a window. He and his family and all the animals longed to be on land once more but only the mountain tops could be seen. Everywhere else was still covered with water and Noah did not dare to open the door.

After waiting a while he let a raven out to see if it could find somewhere to settle. It never came back and after a week Noah sent out a dove. The dove flew around but could find nowhere to rest or find food so it came back to the ark. When Noah saw it fluttering outside, he knew the earth must still be covered with water and he let the bird inside.

Another week he waited with all the animals. Then Noah sent out the dove again and this time it returned in the evening with an olive leaf in its beak. Now Noah knew the waters were really going down. He waited one more week and again sent out the dove. When it did not return Noah knew it was time to leave the ark. He opened the door a crack and in every direction he saw green grass and trees and flowers.

Noah called his family together and all the animals grew quiet to listen to him. "The time has come," he told them. "Now we can leave the ark. Then he and his sons pushed open the great door.

Out poured the animals, squawking and barking, neighing and roaring. Out scampered the mice; out ran the rabbits and hares; out trotted the zebras, the sheep and the horses on to the fresh green grass. Out strode the bears too and the stately lions while the birds sang and fluttered overhead. All the animals were glad to be out in the open once more with room to leap or fly or dance or just to curl up in the warm sunshine.

Then God saw the destruction he had caused and said to Noah:

"I will never again send such a flood. Never again will I destroy all living creatures or curse the land. And as a sign that I shall keep this promise, I give you the rainbow."

Just then a brilliant rainbow arched over the ark and over Noah and his family and all the animals. Ever since that day, whenever the sun comes out in the rain, you will see a rainbow in the sky. It reminds us of God's promise that there will never again be a great flood over the whole earth.